# TEMPLAR, ASSASSINATION, TRIAL & TORTURE
## Nigel Clayton

First Published in Australia by Meni Publishing and Binding in 2009

Copyright © Nigel Clayton, 2009 Templar, Assassination, Trial & Torture

Nigel Clayton asserts the moral right to be identified as the author and owner of this work.



The National Library of Australia Cataloguing-in-Publication data:

Clayton, Nigel. Templar, Assassination, Trial & Torture, 1st ed.
ISBN 978 0 9806585 0 7
1. Templars – Fiction. 2. Crusades – Fiction. 3. Title. A823.4

BISAC
DRA018000    DRAMA / Medieval
FIC009100    FICTION / Fantasy / Action & Adventure
FIC014020    FICTION / Historical / Medieval

Epic Poems by this Author:

Kibeho: An Epic Poem
Afghan - Song of the Desert
Orcinus Orca - Song of the Ocean
Hollandia Nova, 1712 - Song of the Coast

Nigel joined the Australian Army in 1980 at age 17yrs and 2 months, and after completing training at Kapooka was whisked away to the School of Infantry, Singleton, New South Wales, Australia.

He served in the Infantry until injury forced a medical discharge upon him in 1996, after having served in Southeast Asia, 1982; PNG (with the AATPT - Australian Army Training Project Team), in 1990: during the Bougainville Crisis; and in Rwanda, 1995: known world-wide for the Kibeho Massacre which occurred on April 22nd of that year.

He was married in 1999 and has two children.

*One*

25th October, 1314.

The gaoler pushed the knight heavily to the floor and commenced to lock the cell door securely behind him, a sinister smile upon his face, always content in the misery he knew would befall those under his sway.

The dungeon was one of the darkest in France, or supposedly so, but shards of light were adequate enough, and it was by this understanding and predicament that Bernard de Beauvais, Knights Templar, was thankful for the few mercies provided him by nature's gift: he found himself provided the great comfort of a fresh breeze and a fragrance which he couldn't recall, but it did smell quite heavenly: or could he be confused, disorientated and dreaming of things that were.

He lifted his head and sniffed, drawing the fragrance deeply towards his lungs, astounded by how such beauty could be freely provided to him in the settings that now surrounded him.

He was powerless to do anything of his situation and it all seemed rather pathetic and desperate that he should be flung, so carelessly into this cell and predicament, by such greasy hands which likely had never seen a hard day's work conducted or well orchestrated. And the gaoler was careless also, for Bernard had a crust of bread stuffed beneath his shirt to which the gaolers had failed to find during the interval of their haphazard searching of his person. For the gaoler was more concerned for the weapon he carried at his side, and the short knife strapped to his lower leg: which Bernard made sure they found rather too easily in order to take attention from the nourishment that he hid: and a little distraction of his own did provide sufficient aid in his overall deceit.

Bernard pushed his hand into the hiding place of his clothing, his vestment having been stolen from him as his gaolers laughed hysterically. After several seconds he pulled the bread from its hiding and he looked upon it with great satisfaction, being able to make out the outline of his wares but not its poor condition, so pressed as it was: more of a hard biscuit now than anything appealing to the eye. It was then that another prisoner, from the adjoining cell, broke his silence.

"Ahem; I see you have something there," came the crackled sound of an old man, a voice telling the tale of many hours of torture, his nose twitching at a smell he'd not caught for some time, his sight having adapted to the poor light within the dungeon. The very essence of madness strung upon every word: whether hoarse or otherwise, for he was owner of an array, his vocal cords having clearly taken a beating. He'd been sleeping and was now awake, awakened by the shutting of doors as the gaolers made their retreat from the misery within.

The old man staggered to his feet, had trouble gaining secure footing – for he was weak. He was stooping as any old man may stoop, but his stoop was more pitiful and wretched.

Bernard looked up and over to the shifting silhouette of the crouched and hungry man, the shadows - for what they were: poor and hard to see - drifting away, and then the skeleton form of injustice came into full fruition as the blur came upon a small portion of clarity: the barest of light falling their way from a crack within the thick, dungeon door.

Bernard felt sorry for the old man at that moment but had to be more concerned for himself. If he didn't attend to his needs first then he would surely die within the walls of this cell which surrounded him, and he had much thinking to do, much to deliberate upon, and an undernourished body didn't feed the bowls of knowledge any great service by becoming neglected: he'd learnt this during his many years of servitude to his many brothers and religion.

"You look like you haven't eaten for quite some time, old man," said Bernard.

"My name is Aimery, I've been here for two long years," he said. "Less food has passed my lips this past two years as what would have passed in two months on the streets of Paris."

Bernard felt the staleness of the loaf in his hand; its hardness; its lack of essence and contentment. If he kept it all for himself... could he live with that decision? To serve the wretched souls of crusaders and their families, forever and a day; and to pity them all the same...

"Do the years within this… sacred palace, qualify you for a portion of my bread?"

"A single day in this place, palace or not, deserves recognition, let alone a week, a month, or a year," replied Aimery. He licked his lips. "I haven't had good bread in so long that I forget what it tastes like."

"What's the date of your imprisonment, if I may be so bold as to ask?"

"Ah; I can't recall... but it was some time before King Edward's marriage to Isabella of France... daughter of that bastard of a man, King Philip."

Bernard looked into the depths of insanity, the looming forgetfulness of the old man, the obvious dilemma he was in. He stepped forward to grasp a better understanding, to take a better look, to become better learned of this poor creature so painfully stooped before him.

"Then you have been here for six long years," announced Bernard. "Not two." Aimery suddenly found strength within him and his arm was thrust through the bars that separated the two adjoining cells, spittle flying from the jaws of his decaying mouth, the stinking breath of his exhaled gasp falling upon the heavenly knight, as though a beautiful maiden of position had been soiled by mud, or rotten tomatoes, each thrown her way in an attempt to deprave.

"Give me some of that bread, you filthy vermin!" Bernard was suddenly shocked, which was surprising when considering the ordeals that life had thrown at him over the past decades of service to his Order, though nevertheless he stepped back calmly and without due fright, being noble, of great strength and courage.

Bernard stood there silently and arrived upon a mindful decision, for decisions came quick with a man of true wit and fortitude; and he walked over quite casually to the man, for his need was obviously more than his own. Bernard offered the bread, handing it out, his own hand just retrieved from the claws of grasping fingers as Aimery snatched the wares from the man to his front.

Aimery sounded like a hungry beast more than anything else, penetrating noises of hunger coming from deep inside. The food was shoved unceremoniously into his aging mouth, and it lasted but mere seconds before Aimery collapsed upon the floor of his cell with a smile stretched wide across his face.

"I'm glad you can enjoy it," said Bernard. The old man looked up from there upon the floor of his cell.

"Enjoy it! It was like heaven to me. Who are you, to come in here with bread hidden from view, to turn up here with clean skin and clothes that are still fresh from the washing basket?" and spat out a tooth, loosened by his vigorous rage upon the meal made so short.

Bernard looked himself up and down, and although very filthy could see how the old man viewed him differently, for the rags that Aimery wore were falling from around the thin skeleton that they clung so desperately to.

"I'm a knight," said Bernard.

"A knight; hmm; don't look much like a knight to me. You're too old to be a knight; too fat around the face to be a fighting man. Your hair is so grey; and that beard of yours: no knight wears such; you look a disgrace. No; you're too old to be a knight."

"Fat around the face, ah? Maybe it's you who's too thin," said Bernard, and no sooner had the words escaped him and Aimery was back upon his feet, reaching through the bars once more to try and claw at Bernard's flesh.

"You scum, bastard, filthy whore; come closer you shit," spat

Aimery. "You're a homosexual if I ever saw one and should be drawn and quartered for your trouble."

Bernard sat back down upon a wooden bench along the short length of the wall away from the angry man. Bernard could see that he was insane, and he would have to be sure to stay out of his reach, for a crazy man always held much strength and power, even when exhausted through hunger and many years of malnutrition.

"I am a Knights Templar, as true a knight as ever did live." Aimery had settled down once more; quick to temper and quick to console himself. He lifted an ear to the sound of some jingling.

"Hmm, sounds like someone has taken a liking to you, my pet," said Aimery. "The gaoler is coming to see you."

"Maybe he's come to see you."

"No, my dear," insisted Aimery. "It's you he wants."

"Do you always treat your visitors so kindly?" asked Bernard cheekily. "Have you always been so pleasant?"

"You're the first in many months that I've seen," said Aimery. "I've only been brought up here so they can torture me a little, but now it's your turn to dine with the hangman in his chamber of secrets."

"And to think that I've only just arrived," said Bernard, bravely. "How kind of them."

"The man with chains is coming," said Aimery. "He's going to dice you up with the Spanish Tickler; hehehehe." Aimery suddenly changed his tone and his eyes lit up. "That bastard little shit will be here soon. Quick; hide, don't let him see you," and he went scurrying around in circles, looking as mad as he sounded.

The dungeon door burst open and there stood the gaoler with a candle held aloft, his head swaying a little to the left and then right, trying to gain a better look upon the interiors of the cells before him.

"Shut your noise, you little creep, or you'll see the inside of my latest toy."

Aimery suddenly stopped dead in his tracks and stood there, still as a statue, his eyes wide open and looking the gaoler in the face with dumbness pasted across his mad face. "I'll be good," he said.

"You, the knight, get your arse over here," ordered the gaoler as he unlocked the door of bars to Bernard's cell.

A smirk fell over Aimery's face as his eyes locked with Bernard and the knight stepped up to the cell door.

"Move it," said the gaoler as Bernard pushed past and out into the corridor where two strong men grabbed him from either side, the cell door left open, the dungeon door slammed shut and then locked.

"Oh, so be it, to be taken away," said Aimery, mad and demented, twisted in body, mind and soul. "Hehehehe; such a bastard is that gaoler; hmm."

# Two

Bernard was forced along the cold corridors of the castle by those manhandling him, by such bad manner that his security appeared almost secure, and the deadly gloom of his predicament was starting to reveal itself to him as each step faded away. His future was unclear and his innocence assured, but being a Templar was an acknowledgement alone, that a dark future and hangman's noose was but guaranteed.

His mind was alight with further episodes of torture, torture he had endured over the years which had fallen behind him, nothing more than memories which he didn't wish to see again. Tortures issued by the hand of Muslims in forsaken lands, lands which now mused appealing, for at least then he would be breathing fresh air and not this rancid, staleness.

The corridors were lit by torches along its length, a flight of stone steps coming to view and a dungeon door just beside it.

What did the immediate future hold for him? He was a brave man, as brave as any could be, but he still felt like pissing himself, moreso for being forced into spitting upon the cross. The fear of the unknown was knocking loudly upon his consciousness, the likelihood of much pain to fall upon him almost too much to bear, but bear it he would endeavour to do, for to spit on the cross was unthinkable.

All four men entered the torture chamber and Bernard's eyes were immediately filled with dread and worry, though no such look fell upon his face, for he was a player of stakes and held his nerve well, a man known to never panic in a crisis, and this was just that; a crisis born unto the world, to do all it could to melt away the flesh of man. This dreaded palace, this room, this storehouse of the weapons of his gaolers, the weapons of choice that the inquisition relished so much. No matter where he looked the walls were filled with grief and the floor saturated with those heinous devices so prevalent to the torturer's hand.

There was such an assortment of utensils and devices that it boggled the mind, but Bernard was no stranger to the hardships of torture, and previously mentioned, nor the instruments of the profession, but here before him was the largest assortment that he had ever seen. It was as though he'd walked into a museum of artifacts both new and old, a torturer's collection of dreams come true. If he didn't know any better than he would have sworn that what he saw before him was nothing more than a private collection.

And then the reality hit him hard for he could see the blood stains here and there, see where men, women and children, had dined with the gaolers.

"Stand there and don't move," ordered the gaoler and Bernard was released of his restraint as the two men stepped back. "Make a sound and you'll be tortured more than you need to be."

Bernard's eyes wandered around as the gaoler moved before him. No matter where he looked he saw the devices of torture, and when he closed his eyes he saw nothing other than the reminder of the cells in which he had spent much time whilst in the hands of Muslim scum. That brethren of warmongers who invented a religion from a dream, did so in order to combat the Christian belief. And that's all it was, a dream, a religion invented in order to rally the country's troops to oppose the invading West. For men were more apt to die for a cause when told they'd be awarded seventy-two virgins on death. Yes, a brethren of falsehood.

"You see the choices I have; don't you?" said the gaoler, teasing Bernard as he smiled, chuckling a little as the others in the room with him joined in on the jocularity that they were so accustomed to. It meant absolutely nothing to them that such expense should be accosted Bernard, it was nothing to them that this sack of flesh and bone was to meet with a heinous torture.

Bernard was silent. He could feel the evil in these men; he could see that they weren't human. No human tortured a knight of honour: no human tortured women and children, regardless of guilt or innocence.

The gaoler looked to the others and nodded. "You keep your tongue well," he said before punching hard into Bernard's stomach, and the knight doubled over and fell to the floor, banging his head hard against the blood-stained stone. "No one said to kneel; now STAND!"

Bernard did as ordered and the gaoler pointed out some of his favourite instruments of toture. For it would seem, and now confirmed once and for all, by speech alone, that this gaoler would also be his torturer. "I have a Spanish Tickler here, one I know you've heard about," the gaoler was looking for fear, trying to engage the eye of his prisoner to see the terror grow within him; but there was no emotion. Bernard showed good character in the face of such horrendous pain and torture.

"I can strip you naked and rip the flesh from your body bit by bit, without rendering a sweat upon my brow," the gaoler paused, a witless man, and moved over to another toy of his. "And what about this one; do you know what it is? ANSWER ME!"

"An iron box with a concave face," said Bernard. "I don't know that one."

"I place it on your stomach, after you've been restrained upon the cold of the stone floor, and place a rat beneath it... to contain it within; I then place hot coals on top and continue to feed heat upon the surface of the container. The rat becomes agitated and then starts to dig its way through to your spine. It could take several hours for you to die."

"Is that what you want, for me to die?" One of the two men from behind lashed out heavily with his fist to the back of the head and Bernard fell to the ground once more, smashing his face upon the stone, once more: blood came rushing to his nostrils.

"But I prefer this contraption myself," said the gaoler as he moved over to a rack and a foot stock.
Bernard knew what this was: oh yes, he knew this one. It brought a sudden rush of cold that coursed through his body – he knew it well.

"I see the look in your eyes," said the gaoler. "There's no mistaking it." He nodded to his assistants and Bernard was moved with little difficulty over to the rack where he was laid down upon it and his arms were restrained.

There was no noise other than that made by the clanging of chains and the creaking of wood, as Bernard's feet were thrown into the stock and secured.

The gaoler simply looked at Bernard, smiling at him, a small stove of coals moved closer to where the soles of his feet lay bare, a little red flame seen to flicker up from the coals as they continued their process of slow combustion.

The red-hot coals opposite his feet would be screened from doing harm, but whenever the gaoler wished to see pain inflicted he would simply remove the screen of protection and the burning would commence.

"I've seen many men have their feet burnt down to nothing more than a stump, their flesh falling away from charred bone. You have to submit; you have to confess," said the gaoler.

"I can confess to many things," said Bernard, restrained where he lay. "But some things I can't."

"We know what you did in April," said the gaoler. "We know that you killed Pope Clement."

So that was it. The pope. He'd heard of the pope's death.

"You're right," said Bernard, "I confess. I killed the pope and many others like him. Just ask and I'll confess."

The gaoler was stunned, stunned by the seemingly reckless confession. "I see a lie within you," said the gaoler. "Do you think the torture will stop, simply because of your confession?"

"What need do you have to torture the truth from me when the truth has been offered? Sentence me to death and be done with it."

"Ah; no, no, no. We also know of the Battle of Bannockburn."

"Which is understood," said Bernard, for his sacred and most cherished bravado could not go without embellishment - but he was never pretentious; never swaggered. Nevertheless, such legendary action could never go unsung.

"So you confess?"

"I do. Scotland has been good to me."

The gaoler stepped back and looked up to the top of a flight of stone steps and a solitary man stepped out from within the shadows.

# Three

"I am a member of the French Exchequer," said the tall man as he continued on down the flight of steps, very well spoken and obviously well educated. "Would you prefer I speak in French or English?"

"Please," said Bernard. "You can continue in French; I've had enough of the English language due to my stay in Scotland. But I also speak German and Spanish, if either of those should be of aid."

"Ah; a learned man."

"No; just a survivor; a traveller of the world."

The Frenchman continued down and then moved up to be alongside Bernard. He looked Bernard up and down as he laid there.

"What's your name?"

"Bernard de Beauvais, Knights Templar," said Bernard. "Mine is, Guillaume de Blanquefort. You do know that being a Templar is a sin?"

"So I've been advised; hence my fighting for the Scottish."

"And so is killing a pope."

"He deserved it," was this really about the pope? Continue to plead a guilt: do not spit upon the cross.

Guillaume stood over him. "I'm only here to question you. Killing the pope carries severe punishment. Maybe you did it, maybe you didn't."

"I'm going to die anyway, and your inquisition is bent upon more suffering. You wish the Templar to look like the devil worshipers they aren't. If a lie will bring death to fall upon me all the more sooner, so that I can stand beside God in His full glory, then I wish to plead my guilt." Yes; yes; there was an education about this Guillaume. It could be seen by the way he walked; the way he talked; the way he held himself, so proud.

"You can't stand beside God; that's no reward for killing the pope. Also... we are not of the inquisition."

Bernard looked away and saw many chains hanging from pegs upon the dungeon wall. "So be it. I'll not argue with you."

"You don't seem to be afraid," said Guillaume. "You say you committed this terrible crime, a crime against the whole of Europe, not just France. I could give the order right here and now and your feet would be burnt slowly away. I could see to it that the pain you suffer is so great that the Spanish Tickler would be a great relief."

The gaoler looked from one to the other, when the tall man slowly turned to face him and said: "Go, now; take your two men with you."

"But; my orders," protested the gaoler.

"If you don't wish to exchange places with this prisoner, then I suggest you depart this very moment."

The gaoler turned to his companions and moved through the door they'd entered. "And if I hear or see you eaves-dropping then I'll have you all tortured to death. That I promise you. Oh, huh… after I rip out your tongues, of course."

The gaoler and his strongmen wasted not a moment more and scurried away like the vermin they were, almost tripping over themselves with the unveiling of their possible future.

Guillaume waited for the big wooden door to close behind the gaolers and he called upon the others in the shadow above.

Guillaume commenced to untie Bernard's bonds as three other men moved slowly, but purposely, down into the torture chamber, seemingly unperturbed by the place-of-horror in which they now stood. Bernard considered this: they were used to places such as this, or had visited this one in particular, and most recently.

Bernard sat up and rubbed his wrists before curt introductions were made. "Bernard; this is Imbert Bonomel, Ricault Michaelensis, and Johannes Blanke," introduced Guillaume. "By the end of this meeting... we might not be friends, but we'll know enough of one another to consider ourselves... fortunate... I should hope."

There was hopefulness in his voice. This man Quillaume was as though giving praise but it wasn't spoken with a soft or gentle, not even a caring voice. Possibly he was a little bored, or unsettled. He was after something and he may not get it, and that was his fear. He held a fear within that he may be wasting his time. Yes; that was it.

There was a small table and several chairs nearer the centre of the room, where gaolers ate and drank as men were tortured.

"Let's sit and converse," said Guillaume. The men moved over to the small table which had upon it five tumblers and a carafe of water, unnoticed by Bernard until he sat down: not so absurd, really; for the gaoler would have considered these for himself, his two men, Guillaume and… haha…. Something to tease the prisoner with, a refreshment promised but one that would never pass his lips. Bernard stepped towards it. He saw the whips and knots, the rack, the chair, and many other devices for which to bring much suffering upon a man or woman of flesh and bone – did they torture children here too? They must have done. He didn't know the true answer to that, but he knew children were tortured elsewhere, so why not here?

Guillaume had poured four tumblers of water before Bernard snatched out rather hastily, grabbing one and drinking its entire contents. Mmmm, a helpful and considerate man. Guillaume replenished it and Bernard drank half again. He pulled the tumbler away from his lips, both hands wrapped around it, gasping for breath as the water cascaded down his throat, inside and out. He wiped his chin with the back of his hand.

"My three friends and I wish to question you, Bernard, on many subjects. We hope you can shed light upon each with your thoughts and explanations, enlighten us with every aspect of your knowledge and understanding," said Guillaume. "Answer these questions, with every ounce of truth, regardless of what you believe, or what that truth might bring, and you will not suffer a painful death, here in this dungeon, as promised by your gaoler. My job is not to see men tortured, but to see that France is tended to as it should be tended."

Bernard nodded and decided to test them all by speaking out, then and there. "That seems fair enough; a little water to quench my thirst and a few answers to quench yours."

Bernard simply smiled as Guillaume asked: "Shall we make

a start?"

"Please," replied Bernard. "You have my undivided attention." and he was most, most very, extremely eager to learn of where this was leading.

"I could start by questioning you on the death of the pope, but I won't insult the intelligence of my friends, instead I'll simply advise you that Pope Clement died a little over a month after Molay, and two small books covered with tanned leather, each with an iron lock and containing the rules of the Templar, were found in his bedchamber. He held high regard and much respect for the Templar Order."

"As I'm sure the pope did," replied Bernard.

"Do you believe in the call of 1095, when Pope Claremont gave the call for the murderous Saracens, so evil and dirty, to be rid of this world?"

"I do," replied Bernard. Guillaume waited several seconds.

"Is that your answer, no extension?"

That was almost comical in itself, thought Bernard. This man was after a story. "I do believe, with all my heart, for the world to be rid of the Saracen scum."

Guilluame had a slight smirk upon his face. Bernard saw a little sarcasm [possibly] but continued with the answering of the questions.

"Do you stand by the call for Holy War, by all the Christian states of Europe, to go with arms into the Holy land?"

"I do," said Bernard, and not waiting for a lifting of Guillaume's eyebrows in search of an 'extension', offered this: "I too, answered the call. Rescue was the call, rescue the poor souls of their demise and starvation, and rescue the holy places of Palestine from the filthy hands of the Mohammedans as they clasped their scimitars in foolish effort to rid the world of God. Yes; I served."

Bernard took another drink of water. "It's good."

"Are you the true hero you claim to be or a misguided fool that represents what was once a formidable force of knights dressed in white; or were you a simple coward?"

Bernard could hold his tongue and temper, had little choice right now, but this so-called Guillaume was pushing his luck, accusing him of cowardice. And his eyes flickered here and there. He saw other instruments of torture around; those that could crush a man's fingers and toes, another to crush the skull, and furthermore, a device which could be placed into an orifice and then force that orifice open, where a red-hot poker could then be placed within, to burn the bowels of any poor creature from the inside-out.

"I am not a coward. I served with honour," said Bernard. "And neither have I, at any time in the past, ever claimed to be a hero." But this did not mean that men of good deeds and standing did not feel proud. To have that feeling of being honorable but not display it for the world to see.

"Being a Knights Templar is to claim such rights, is it not?"

"That's not how I see it," answered Bernard. "Any man can be a hero; such status isn't issued simply because of one's transition from peasant to knight."

"You; a peasant?"

"Most people I've met, of humble beginnings, hide behind a facade of wealth and position; they don't serve God," answered Bernard in all truthfulness. "It is the peasants of this world who serve God, not for personal wealth, but for the fortunes of others, so that they too, will feel the blessed love of Christ. They, each and every one, share their beliefs and belongings as best they can. A wealthy man will turn a beggar away, for fear of unintentionally inviting a swarm, but a poor man will allow one to bed down in his stable, despite the fear of having his good horse stolen in the middle of the night."

"Then how is it that you present yourself, either willing or not, to the front of this court—"

"Court!?"

Guillaume was stumped by the harshness of the reply and almost forgot himself: almost forgot his purpose. "You are here before me this day, with your skin still intact and not a wound or scar to be seen anywhere upon your body?"

Bernard looked from one to the other and revealed the scars so prevalent upon him, removing his garments so that those before him could see the scars of torture across his chest and back, of the scars of battle upon his left shoulder and down his right thigh, and then of the scars upon the soles of his feet where he was once treated as all other Templars before him had been treated.

Guillaume was once again stumped, but the look of shock that fell upon him, even if temporarily, soon vanished. And the other three men saw the pain which had been inflicted upon Bernard and each felt a measure of guilt within.

"A story to tell, you might have, but as to whether or not it's to be believed, I can't say," said Guillaume.

"That's not a question, but I can answer it," said Bernard, for he had quickly learned to embellish his short replies with colourful stories - as we have already noted.

# *Four*

And good memories recall the past.

The episodes of war that preceded the fall of Acre were heinous.

The population of Acre at the time of its displacement was estimated at 40,000 souls, which included 15,000 soldiers, most of whom were siege workers, heroes one and all, men volunteering for work where wages couldn't be secured; but there were also the unscrupulous.

Men, who served as soldiers, whether they were siege workers or not, never served without the promise of good wages to accompany their efforts, unless such service was for God, and it is here that we understand their clear thinking and consideration, for a promise of entry into heaven had been provided to them, one and all: and yet so many fled.

The lead up to the fall of Acre was one of turmoil, a path of destruction and poor politics having laid the future for the grand city; set in stone was its destiny.

Bernard understood all there was to know of Acre for he had lived there for many years, having served pilgrimages during the long journey across land and sea to the Holy land, and again upon the walls of cities under siege by the vermin

Mohammedans, all pressing hard to rid the desert and coastline of Christian presence. But nowhere else, more than Acre, did he find his true purpose in life: but that was in the near future, far from his current station.

And so where do we start? But of course; Tripoli; yes, yes; that was the place.

Bohemond VII had died in October of 1287 and with his passing went the transition of rule to his sister, Lucia, who tempted no effort [for effort tempted sweat - it was far better to conduct politics 'the ladies way'] to seat herself upon the land of Tripoli. She remained in Italy to the dissatisfaction of many, the leaders in the vicinity of Tripoli seeing no good reason as to why they should accept the rule of one so far from Tripoli's borders. It was with a great amount of heart-felt contempt that the position was hence given to Sibylla of Armenia who immediately moved to place Bishop Bartholomew, the Bishop of Tortosa, into a seat of great power, a contempt felt by every Knights Templar across the face of the known world. And so Lucia had lost her rule, dropping it so unceremoniously from the service tray handed her.

A year later, Lucia arrived upon the scene to claim it for her own, Tripoli in all its glory, but the newfound power of its self-rule was not something that could be so easily washed away and so war ships of the Genoese, on accepting Tripoli as a trading partner, being a protectorate, were herald to the area to defend it against any naval force that might otherwise try to unload troops loyal to Bohemond's sister upon the piers and streets of the city.

The Templars were in no two minds as to where their loyalty stood... with the Venetians; and it was well known that the

Knights Templar had built much of their naval force with the help of labour from the Venetians, harnessing their great ability in ship building to suit their needs and desires.

Amidst this tension there was much trouble in Tripoli, squabbling and fighting, Genoese against the Venetians, and so a secret meeting was held in Egypt where Sultan Kalaun saw the disruption in the city as an opportunity not to be missed. He saw plans within a plan and wasted no time in putting his visions into action, for what good was a vision if not acted upon, and whether they were simple, mindless dreams, or concoctions from somewhere more lofty and beyond the grave, he did not know, but act he must surely do.

By March of 1289, just seventeen months after Bohemond's death, there were 10,000 Muslim soldiers surrounding the city, and Venetian and Genoese alike forced aside their differences for the most part, but there was always a skirmish or two upon the wall and within the city streets between men that were not-so-happy nor content with the situation at hand. They quickly saw to it that the evacuation of the city's treasure was undertaken and the populace placed on board their galleys: this being put into immediate effect on things turning rotten.

As with any other siege, the sounds of battle filled the air, Kalaun giving the order for an immediate assault to take place as news reached his ears that a great mass of supplies were being drawn into the holds of galleys at port. He wouldn't permit the wealth of Tripoli to escape his grasp. What was the point in capturing a city when it was empty of gold and treasure? Slaves? Yes, yes, there were slaves to be had, but wealth was all important, especially where an army needed to be maintained.

There was little significance here on relics, books and art being procured for museums and libraries, no; no, of course not; that was ridiculous; it was wealth; wealth and land. And even for a city worn down by siege, there was great worth in its future, for what wealth in trade may be lost now, could be won again in the very near future. Every country in the world relished trade. But what if Tripoli were turned to ashes, every stone ground to dust? What if this grand city was torn to its very foundations?

The galleys saw the attack coming, heard the people screaming, and saw the smoke from fires erupt from within the city walls. There was mayhem and panic like so few had ever seen before, and this was just the beginning of a nightmare to last. War drums filled the air with dread; catapults filled it with volley after volley of rock, prisoners and large blocks of stone, all employed as rubble: and a cow appeared as though to fly momentarily through the air, used as a means to bombard the heathen. The galleys fled and the citizens that remained looked on with an overwhelming weight of fear falling upon them, for themselves, for their children, but rarely for their neighbour. But the knights, they were different, for all populace were like a child to them.

Bernard looked on as the last of the ships left the port, a large rock from a siege weapon missing it by mere whiskers, a great splash of water surging up and over those nearer the bow of the vessel. The sound of the battle horns filled his ears, hardly drowned out by the actions of battle themselves, lofty calls from horns for troops to move here and there.

Raoul de Jay and Brian de Gizy looked at Bernard, their faces filled with grief, dirty and worn thin. They were brothers,

Knights Templar.

"Bernard," said Raoul, hardly lifting his voice, as though it was too much effort for him this day, no sign of panic displayed, only honour and courage and discipline. "The Muslim scum have stormed the walls."

"It won't be long now," added Brian, stroking his palm subconsciously against the hilt of his weapon, as though a warning to his beloved that blood would soon be spilled: It shall have a sheath of blood, not leather.

"We'll have to meet them head on," issued Bernard. "Give aid to the citizens of Tripoli where aid can be given, be their shield, protectors true."

"We'll not live through this," said Raoul. "But, by God, I'm willing. And by the graces of God, when I should fall, the gates of heaven will open to me and allow ready access,"

"Me, too," added Brian. "I shall want some of that action and just reward."

"We'll do our duty, to the citizens of Tripoli and to God," said Bernard. He looked again out to sea, the fleet of treasure, blood and bone, making for safety where safety could be sought. And then something quite despicable caught his eye, something that stagnated upon his mind, of a despicable action as any he'd witnessed. "I see before me a sad sight. I see our marshal departing, Marshal de Vanadac and Lucia."

"Fear not the sod," said Brian. "De Modaco is here amongst us."

"Ordered us to death, more like," said a seemingly deflated Raoul, though nothing further from the truth could exist, for he was as brave as the others. Would he, though, denounce an order to retreat? Not if it meant further calamity for the enemy at large.

"The treasure has gone, the city is worthless," said Brian of the clear and obvious predicament, highlighting more for himself than for any other the probable outcome of all within, of all the poor citizens to be caught as though by netted traps.

Bernard looked at them both sternly. "This city is far from worthless. There are many men, women and children, needing much aid. I won't allow myself to stand by and see a child torn from its mother's bosom whilst blood passes through my veins."

The calamity of the city under assault filled their ears more so than before. The walls shook, the floor vibrated beneath their feet, the smell of smoke wafted upon the breeze as it went freely about, as though not a care in the world; and a bird flew past: what did a bird know of war and misery, what was the noise of battle to him? The fires created by war and siege were probably less to him than a forest caught on fire by lightning strike. "It's time," said Bernard, forcing the play of his mind. "Time for us to draw our swords and disappear into the folds of fury that approach us this moment in time, time to deal a meagre punishment upon this ugly thorn ."

"I hear you," said Brian. "Shall we fight side-by-side, just one last time?"

"We shall," said Bernard as he drew his sword from its sheath and stepped off briskly towards the sound of women screaming. The three men no longer looked upon the sea, no longer able to view the galleys making good their escape, and together they came face-to-face with their foe. Scimitar clanged with sword, parry met by slash, stab made against the flesh of the enemy as the battle grew thick around them.

The Templars were but few in number, too few to make a difference, a small garrison when compared to what had fled, for the Knights Templar weren't familiar with fleeing a battle, when the citizens under their charge were seeking the mercy of the enemy, a mercy which would never be granted. So their marshal had vacated with Lucia, what did it matter, so long as the long arm of the contingent did its duty and continued to serve God in the best way it could?

Blood cased the ground of the city, everywhere they looked was death, and easily seen was the destruction, the effects of a siege turned bad, a city where plunder and rape was now the order of the day. Muslim men went from door to door and killed the men they encountered, sparing half the women they found to fill the shackles they carried, and children old enough to work in the mines were taken away as slaves.

Brian and Raoul were slaughtered, and when finally the fighting within Bernard came about it was by the blurring of his eyes, from exhaustion and the loss of blood. Bernard was taken prisoner; he'd collapsed after killing many men, having served his God once more. Yes indeed, He'd lost much blood in his efforts to save the innocent. He had deep wounds to both his left shoulder and right thigh, injuries that would heal with time but leave a heinous scar, scars which would freely feel the pains of life unless massaged prior to strenuous activity: in particular where the weather was foul, more particular as old age approached from within the folds of darkness, forever unknown until there at your front, unveiling itself as a foregone conclusion: a foregone future.

And so he awoke to find himself lying upon a bench, arms

tied back, below the rim of that on which he was strapped, his feet secured fast, tied together at the end of the bench, hanging over the edge. And it became clear to him that he'd been woken by a splash of seawater upon his face, for the stinging of salt upon his shoulder wound made it quite clear: not to mention the taste of salt upon his tongue as several droplets rendered themselves unnecessarily admissible upon his upper lip.

Bernard's eyes slowly opened, the daze clearing from his foggy mind, a sourness coming upon his head, the backs of two men seen, not far in front of him, as he looked around with effort.

He was in a darkened room, an echo heard from somewhere behind his head, but he couldn't see. His eyes flickered, he was coming around fully.

The two Muslim men turned simultaneously, both speaking in their foreign tongue, and then another drew up alongside them, a torturer who was there to see his duty fulfilled, rubbing his hands together for the excitement which was to become his way once more, and for the glory of Allah, and the glory of Muhammad and his thirteen wives, he would see his duty done.

The torturer addressed Bernard. "I am, Mohammed," said the man, a scar on his cheek, his face dark and sculptured thin. "I'm going to defeat you; by the heat of my cauldron, with oil placed upon the soles of your feet. I'll see to it you're softened in heart and hardened under foot, charring you like burnt meat."

"No questions; no search for information?" asked Bernard, still feeling the effects from loss of blood, a little blurry in the eye, his gaze coming and going: possibly a good thing, considering he was to be tortured.

"That will come, but first I must have my pleasure," said Mohammed as he commenced to plaster oil upon the soles of Bernard's feet, to the joy of the other two who looked at one another and smiled.

"You enjoy your work, I see," said Bernard.

"Save your tongue, Templar, or I'll burn it out," and with that said he removed the small shield between Bernard's feet and the open flames and burning coals, and the heat radiated out immediately. So fast was this torturer, so eager he seemed to be at his work; maybe the torture would be short [but not sweet], death incurred haphazardly but all the more welcome in the eyes of Bernard.

Bernard's toes moved with the suddenness of the heat and within the time it took him to draw ten breaths the discomfort displaced by the build-up of heat had commenced to take effect. The muscles around his face contracted as he felt his skin burning upon the soles of his feet.

And so the screams of pain and torture erupted from within Bernard as the soles of his feet were burnt to within a hair's width of his becoming permanently handicapped, and the shield was suddenly replaced, and over several minutes of time passing so fast, a little relief was felt.

The door to the room then burst inwards and a man approached the torturer, speaking loudly but not understood by Bernard.

"Stop the torture," yelled the appointed keeper.

"I've not yet started; only burnt his skin away is all," answered Mohammed, annoyed by the interruption, eager to continue with his work.

"We've secured a ransom," said the keeper. "Don't harm him any further; he's to be released; by order of the Sultan. His better condition will net a larger sum."

Mohammed turned to the sweating form of shattered life upon the bench and moved closer. "You can count your blessings, one and all," said Mohammed. "A ransom has been paid for your release... and just when I was starting to enjoy myself."

# Five

Bernard collapsed before his rescuers as they stood before the persons of the Sultan's council of prisoner-exchange, little said as man-of-flesh was replaced by a purse of gold coin, and out upon the field around them, where the desert could be seen stretched out as far as the eye could see, several dozen other men were moved along.

Bernard was carried away in silence with the aid of two strong men. "Give my thanks to the Sultan for his efforts in this exchange," said Guy. "If it was in my power I'd request the release of all the citizens of Tripoli."

"Give us Acre and you can have them," came the Muslim response.

"I can't currently commit to such an exchange," replied Guy to the sour wit of the scum to his front. "You've already raised Tripoli to the ground; what would you have in store for Acre? Much the same, I would fear."

"And fear is what you'll feel if the Sultan's clemency isn't accepted."

Guy turned to leave but said one more thing. "I leave it to those of importance to seek an audience with the Sultan. Anything is possible."

"And possibilities are few."

# Six

Guillaume stood up and paced across the stone floor before turning with further questions, facing Bernard as he sat behind the small table in the centre of the floor.

"We're talking about the end of the crusades; the loss of Tripoli and the loss of Acre. The crusades appear lost... there seems little point in tending the venture any further. It seems so easily given away, the defences of Acre given so easily to the enemy, as was Tripoli, as though handed over upon a platter. Why should your story be so boldly believed? So you have scars upon your body, feet that resemble the hide of a rhinoceros or worst."

"I can only attest to my efforts by filling your ears with dread," said Bernard.

"Yes; dread that we see every day of our lives," replied Guillaume, seemingly waving aside the hideous scars carried by Bernard.

"It's for the king and the pope to decide on the fate of the crusades. It's not for me to question the deliberate withdrawal from Tripoli, or Acre; me, a common man," said Bernard.

"A Knight; a Templar," corrected Guillaume. "You're not a common man. No man who wears a red cross can be considered as just a man. And so I'm faced with the torments of making a few decisions; as to whether to believe you or not. But you are not a common man."

"I fought to protect all that was Tripoli; its walls, its streets, its people; and I thought even harder still, knowing well the ways of torture, to protect all within the walls of Acre, said Bernard. "I don't care whether you believe me or not, but I care for my service to God and His people.

"Yes; Acre," said Guillaume as he sat back down, the other men in the room silent and listening, taking note as the questioning continued, and for what purpose; Bernard didn't yet know.

"And of all the crusades into the holy land there comes one which was of all-mighty importance," continued Guillaume, "and that was the last, when Acre, being surrounded on all sides, was attacked so feverishly by the Mamluks of Egypt. A great calamity it was for all those of the Christian faith, in the year of our Lord, 1291. Were you there as you claim to have been; were you, in body and soul, present upon the battlefield and the bastions of Acre when the time arrived for it to be smashed of Christian semblance, when all good men fled Syria, the last Christian post, and where the Latin Kingdom was hence, lost to the world of scimitar-wielding scum?"

"You seem content enough to place the blame on me, accusations that fall well short of purpose," said Bernard.

"You gave up the fight, you gave up the city, just like the Knights Templar gave up the fight in Tripoli," said Guillaume, testing Bernard, making him feel sick to the stomach with the accusations of cowardice.

"Back in Acre, after Tripoli was lost and raised to the ground, there was a great amount of shock and fear," said Bernard. "It's as though the entire Muslim race had reached out and strangled us, one and all."

Bernard took a deep breath. "Each and every one of the inhabitants of Acre had previously assumed that their trading with the Muslims was so steadfast and secure that safety had been purchased and could weather the test of time itself."

Bernard took another drink of water from his tumbler and placed it back down again. "But King Hugh felt differently about the situation as did the growing anxiousness within the city streets and churches," continued Bernard. "The king sent a messenger to the pope and the monarchs of Europe, requesting military aid and protection, protection from what was seen as a great calamity brewing upon the horizon. But the request for aid fell upon deaf ears and with it the restlessness of the good citizens of Acre grew and grew."

"And what else did you see; what else do you think we should hear of the state of Acre before it was handed over upon a platter for Sultan Kalaun to do with as he wished?" said Guillaume.

"There was a great quarrel and much fighting amongst them; the Guelfs and Ghibellines; Pisans and Genoese; all of those wearing a different armour of flesh sought to bring harm upon the other. It was as though the devil himself had risen from the ground to swallow up all semblance of society, to swallow up all that was good in men. And then came what at first appeared to be a little reprieve when twelve thousand mercenary were sent to help maintain order and give protection once more to a city in threat of extinction," Bernard looked down upon the table, took a mouthful of water, looked up to the chains hanging upon the walls of the cold room and then continued. "There were entirely untested and unskilled men, an army that wasn't fit to be called an army, made up of Italians who had no skills or options for other employment, and peasants who hardly knew how to employ a hoe, let alone a sword."

"You were once a peasant, a man of little value," said Guillaume; a statement: not a question being voiced.

"I'm not wrong," said Bernard. "Some men... some peasants are not men, some have no skills but squander what they can from their land. But I was able to learn. I was taught the value of honesty and hard work."

"I too know of the men sent to Acre," said Guillaume, "but find it hard to believe how such unrest could still be invested by Acre, even in the face of accepting an untested army of peasants."

"The Venetians had invested much in Acre and were happy to transport the army within the holds of their most excellent fleet, but had they known what was to fall upon the city streets then they would have been more wary," said Bernard.

He continued. "The army of peasants began to rob the citizens and businesses of Acre, taking from the merchants of the city all they had, the peasants doing as they wished to all of those that stepped before them. There was much chaos and uncertainty. They drank and got drunk, spent time in the pleasure of prostitutes instead of on the walls or on the streets maintaining good order. One morning a huge fight broke out and the treaty with the Saracens was shattered once and for all, with the murder of many Muslims taking place."

"And why wasn't order restored by the Knights Templar?" asked Guillaume.

"We were vastly outnumbered," said Bernard. "What could we do?"

"Ah, I see," said Guillaume. "And so you did the same when the Muslim assailed the city, being outnumbered and nowhere to go, and so you gave up the fight, handed over the city."

"When Christian fights Christian, it's hard to pick a side: I am not a juror, I cannot say what injustice is unless plainly seen. It's different, in every respect. Defending citizens from within a secure location is easier to conduct than when twelve thousand are running around freely, doing as they please. It's like a melee, being surrounded by fights of man against man; all you can do is defend yourself. Hard it is for one man to fight against ten, even if behind a barricade, but easier it is for ten men upon a rampart to defend against one hundred. There is safety in numbers, and security to be obtained from heavy fortification."

Guillaume wasn't entirely happy with the response. "It would seem a miracle in itself that the Hospitaller Knights could retain Cyprus and Rhodes, such fledgling lands amidst the turmoils of sea, to defend against galleys galore, and yet you could not, even with a great wall to defend you."

Guillaume looked to his comrades and saw one of them scribing away in his book. "They served – and still do – as a barrier to ward off the Muslim expansion right across the Mediterranean, and yet you sit before us here and claim that such heroic efforts are pittance when compared to the efforts of the Knights Templar, and that Acre could not be saved," argued Guillaume. "I find it all very hard to believe."

"History doesn't always record the fighting that men do," said Bernard. "I see your fellow brothers here, scribing freely what they hear, recording all for the prosperity of man, but where are such men when there is fighting to be done?"

Bernard felt as though he had just then accused them but continued on. "There was a riot of the sorts you have never seen before, citizens taking sides, fighting against those they considered to be the weakest, standing against those of a different nationality – there are many reasons why one chooses to fight alongside others."

Bernard paused for a moment before continuing. "And where does this leave us all, but with many dead Muslims littering the streets of Acre, and the families of the deceased wanted nothing more than sweet revenge, for justice to be delivered. Mercenaries are not men, are not brave, are not deserving of the wages they secure, nor the pillages of war which fall to within their dirty, muggy grasp. You would be better to equip murderers and thieves with swords and knives and tell them to help themselves to the sheep and their lambs. It would have been better to have kept the peasant army as far away from Acre as possible."

"Or better still that the Knights Templar had intervened upon this… unwelcomed scourge of misery; this deception, fraud: this pack of wolves," finished Guillaume. "We all know that Sultan Kalaun requested the guilty to be handed over for the wanton murders they committed, and that the Venetians were opposed to this; we are also aware of the army that Kalaun commenced to gather in earnest, but what we don't know is what action, or actions, were taken by the templar to help defend the city."

"First and foremost," said Bernard, "we argued that the guilty should be turned over, that those guilty of murdering Muslims should be dealt with, but the Venetians were opposed to this as were the citizens of Acre. I cannot agree with this, despite my good opinion of Venetians. The city was large; one pocket of citizens did not necessarily know of the treatment suffered by others further away. Hard to believe, I know, but this is one of the realities of life in Acre, as it is with life in Constantinople."

Guillaume could see the anguish in Bernard's eyes as the knight continued. "It's hard to protect a city when a city refuses to be defended. Our Grand Master, de Beaujeu, put forward his strategy to try and maintain security but the citizens felt that we were doing nothing more than trying to protect our wealth, our growing financial interests," Bernard scoffed at the thought, thinking it ridiculous that the citizens of Acre could have been so stupid or mistaken. "The citizens looked upon us in scorn: they may as well have accused us outright and called us cowards to our faces as opposed to behind our backs," said Bernard. "Our first step towards the security of Acre was washed aside by the guilty, by those citizens that had come together to murder the Muslims of a once peaceful city. They said that we had turned our backs upon the Christian faith. You can't protect those that don't want to be protected," insisted Bernard. "You cannot argue a point of fact if the point is blunted in any way, and when a few are outspoken by a vast many then there is little hope of your voice being heard. De Beaujeu did all he could to warn the Venetians and he saw quite clearly behind the hidden guise of Kalaun: an army was on the move. Assistance was requested from the Venetians and they then turned their backs upon us and scolded us, refusing to support us in our move to defend the citizens of Acre as a whole. I don't know if this was due to cowardice and their own interest, or whether or not they were simply opposed to law and order. Wealth is a greed on its own, and much greed did these mercenaries have."

"Yes; the Venetians may have made a mistake, but such mistakes shouldn't hold a man hostage. You can see their point, however," said Guillaume. "I've heard you talk of your comrades – and whether they be considered brothers or not, is not for me to prove or disprove. I see the Venetians' point of view, of the Knights Templar and their failure, their inability to correctly furnish and support the holy wars, but collect your dues you do so easily, and from the poor peasants of Europe who can no better afford a loaf of bread than to pay for the services you claim to have provided, where protection is guaranteed. Where is such a guarantee now that the walls of Acre have been breached and the poor souls lay across the mat of the desert, littering it like the flies cover the fresh excrements of a dog's rear-end?"

"And yet you see before you the very privileges of the crusades, those privileges which have been bestowed and showered upon you and your king and your country," said Bernard. "Europe has learnt much and prospered from every drop of Templar blood that has been spilt upon the desert, every drop allowed to fall upon the stone blocks of walls they've defended right across the known world."

"After almost two hundred years of salvation and glorious accomplishment, Acre is given up as though a worthless piece of ground, the Holy land to be turned over and currently remains in

Muslim hands. The Turks now have a free reign to make good advance upon Constantinople due to the sourly efforts mustered by you and your men," said Guillaume. "The Emperor is sure to be soiling his robes this very moment, for the likes of you and your pitiful efforts in saving the face of Christendom and Acre."

Guillaume stood up and commenced to pace around. "The crusades were not furnished for the purpose of seeing the good citizens of Europe being ground into the soil like forgotten thieves are cast into the dungeons of our correction facilities, but were cast from the graces of the pope and other great men like him, acting in good faith for the voice of heaven, to defeat the Saracen at every turn; not for one as yourself to make good wage..."

"There is always more to the story than can be seen!" shouted Bernard before lowering his tone once more. "You weren't there; you have only heard stories from others who have heard stories. Melot Sapheraph, Sultan of Babylon, had gathered together a mighty host, and reached the city of Acre without any resistance, because of their quarrels with one another, cutting down and putting to waste all the vineyards and fruit trees, and all the gardens and orchards, which were most lovely thereabouts."

"Did you see the orchards, did you see it all with your own eyes?" asked Guillaume.

"I did," answered Bernard, seemingly proud of it, as though a worldly accomplishment. He paused for a moment and saw that the others were waiting. "Shall I tell my story?"

"We're waiting," replied Guillaume.

"When, William de Beaujeu, the Master of the Templar, a

very wise and brave knight, saw the calamity that was growing before him, he feared that the fall of the city was at hand. It was all due to the quarrels of the citizens. He took counsel with his brethren about how peace could be restored; he did this before going out to meet the Sultan, who was a very special friend of my Master's, to ask him whether they could, by any means, repair the truce which had been broken between them."

# Seven

Bernard rode out with others of the Order, to meet with Sultan Kalaun, the measure of pressure placed upon the soles of his feet by the stirrups rather irritating and uncomfortable: yet, you had to be alive to feel discomfort, and so, in a strange way, this pain was good.

They went unmolested by the many soldiers that stood and sat about, eating and drinking, preparing for battle, watching them pass by nervously: but a nervous stare was not necessarily due to poor nerve: a look of… intimidation, loafing, surprise, conflict, or the simple shock of seeing Templar Knights ride by so casually: but the army that surrounded them was very small in comparison to what would soon be. If these people were nervous, by any degree, it would not be for long. And heaven forbid what was to become. But all good men know that once a battle has commenced, nerve is strengthened, fear is honourably lifted as thou by some miracle. Was this the faith in God that each and everyone held within, or was it God's work? Did God give courage to men that needed it, regardless of what name that God went by? Muhammad was wise in the creation of his vision.

Bernard looked around from atop his horse as their mounts took them further into the concentration of tents further afield, but it wasn't far to the Sultans tent where they were to have a parley, where an exchange of ideas and negotiations were to be enacted out and offered between men of opposing armies. Bernard could only guess as to what would happen; and he was seldom wrong or disappointed. He had learnt many things over the years and his time as a Knights Templar was just and rewarding. He'd learnt many things, yes indeed, and one of those abilities was the reading of a man's mind portrayed by the movement of the body, a language spoken in unison with speech, a combination combined to form a truth.

The six Templars, alongside their leader, dismounted and walked up to the seated form of Kalaun who had beside him an entourage of bodyguards and native girls bearing fruit and water. It would seem that not a luxury was missing. The lines of communication, administration, and supply chains must be most worthy. Such a sustenance of order and maintenance could see a siege held for many years to come, but no king or commander of men wished to prolong the inevitable: how unregrettably costly that could be. No; a long siege would not do justice to either side, and so it was peace or immediate... destitution.

Kalaun was not fluent in French but he had by his side another that was, an interpreter who received no introduction, for he was used primarily and foremost as a tool by Kalau: one does not introduce a pet unless that pet is bred to show, and an interpreter is not to be seen, only to be heard.

Kalaun got to his feet and moved forward, exchanging a hand grip with the Master of the Templar, a meek smile upon his lips, a most friendly character to be sure. It would be easy to read such a man, for men of this calibre were never afraid to voice the truth. A man of this calibre almost always listened to another's point of view, even if such a view was to be cast aside as ridicule: as rubbish.

Further exchange of welcome and thanks was given, as is the formality of such exchanging of negotiations, before the six knights in front of the Sultan were offered water to drink and something exotic to eat. William gave his approval. All but two knights waved thanks to the offer of something to eat, but all freely accepted the water and drank a little before placing the drinking vessels aside.

"I wish to assure you that I want nothing more than to see the siege upon Acre lifted, and I will do all I can to ensure that good relations continue between us," voiced William de Beaujeu. "Your men are few and could be easily parried; even expelled from the land; but the last thing I wish to do is to test our great friendship."

"I'm a little disappointed that it took such disruption for us to meet again after so long, old friend," said the sultan through the interpreter. "I, too, wish to see our friendship remain intact. But to quibble on the size of my army would herald little, if any, conviction or thought of withdrawal, I'm sure."

"It's been a long time," replied William as he smiled, allowing the introductory 'size versus size' be forgotten; at least for the moment.

"It has indeed," and then straight the point of the matter, no delusion, no trickery of art or displacement: facts are facts and serve all purpose. "I needn't remind you that I'm aware of the city's state of affairs, of the squabbling that takes place between the inhabitants, of their growing nervousness," said the Sultan, wiping the smile from Beaujeu's face.

And to this Bernard could see that the Muslims of Acre were as free with tongue as they were with their desire to spread their religion. Was it possible that the murder of Muslim citizens within Acre was a good thing? A spy less could reap large reward. Maybe the Venetians were right, afterall: maybe it was the Venetians who organised the murdering of the Muslims within Acre.

"It grieves us all," said William, looking around at the others. "But all that can be done, has been done. Those responsible for such heinous acts will be tried."

But being tried was not reward enough. "The many dead, Muslims slaughtered and cast from Acre bring much misery to bear upon me," continued Kalaun. "But with all that has happened there is still only one thing that I really wish for, and that is the city of Acre, to secure it for all Muslims. See fit to hand it over and I'll allow all of its citizens to depart unarmed. I'm not interested in slaves or slaughter. It's not for me to kill the innocent. What sits on Muslim land simply belongs to us and us alone. You are here in this country as unwarranted guests, but I shall… waiver all poor treatments of the past, and quite happily, the intrusions of all Christians, as a simple error of good judgement," again he smiled. "Our friendship should be maintained for future generations, and so leave now and be done with all hate."

"What you ask is much," replied William, "but might be possible if I'm given time to ensure that your request is passed on appropriately. People find it hard to leave behind a home well furnished with love. A city has a character which can seldom be worn by another, but in time we shall depart in good measure and form, but much time is needed. I ask this of you, my friend."

The sultan nodded, though none could tell if it was in agreement with what William had said or simply an acceptance of William's position and his responsibilities to those that he both commanded over and served.

And then came the acceptance of notion, by offering a counter, to embellish the ridicule so readily gifted by the knight in white. "I would also insist that a single sequin be paid me for every single person within the city," said Kalaun. "For this you may all go free. Call it a meagre tax of export if you so desire."

"I'll pass the information on," said William.

"I pray that my terms will be accepted," said the Sultan. "I'm a generous man, but if my terms aren't met then I'll see to it that Acre is taken by force. An army is being gathered on the horizon and will be here very soon. The blood of every single Christian within Acre will be on your hands."

Could this be true, could there be an army on the horizon? This Sultan was well informed and organised, so yes; yes… yes thrice, it was quite reasonable for such an army to appear at any moment. William nodded in acknowledgement of the terms and together with his men rode back to the city of Acre. No sooner was the gate barred, and portcullis lowered, and William turned to face the men that had accompanied him to see the Sultan.

"We need to gather the leaders of this great city, to pass on the terms offered by Sultan Kalaun. If the terms aren't met then bloodshed will follow. Don't release any information of the negotiations on the terms offered by the Sultan before they are gathered, otherwise they might be persuaded to send a representative instead of themselves, and I need each leader present to press home the importance of fulfilling the Sultan's offer. Bernard, see to it that all leaders are called forth; have them attend the castle of the Templars this evening."

"Yes, Master William; immediately," complied Bernard as he went to fulfil his duty.

# Eight

"So far," said Bernard to Guillaume, "I would say that I served the Order well."

"I won't argue against the fact that you seemed to have served in accordance with the Grand Master's wishes, but it still doesn't forgive the surrendering of Acre; it was so much that was fought for... lost forever."

"There was no surrender... not in the end."

"Surrender is surrender, whether at the initial stages of the siege or later on; whether late or early: Should a Templar change its spots to suit the hour of the day, as a common feline may its desire, to acquire change and need. The cusp of desire was there, to puncture and bleed, to infest the minds of those wishing to take the city by force: your actions, or those of your master, through you, saw to that.

"The Grand Master did all he could under the weight of decision and requirement. My father once had a saying, that two peas cannot share a pod but apples and oranges must learn to live together," said Bernard. "There was no room for Christian rule and that or the heathen, but that should not prevent the two sharing what Acre had to offer. And so the Master passed on the terms of the sultan and was very explicit in all that he passed on, including his own views, and his own confidence, that all would be permitted to depart Acre with their possessions."

"Please, tell us all here today, what happened next?" said Guillaume, eager to hear from a lion's mouth, for he'd only read reports, never heard the story form one so close to the truth.

"The Grand Master was labelled a coward by everyone in the city, not just the leaders of those that populated the last semblance of Christian faith within such a harsh land so far from home; but I tell you now, he only sought to save the lives of all citizens," and Bernards deflating tone appeared to raise the brow of those accosting him so openly, namely the instigator of challenges, Guillaume.

"You sound defeated... tired of being away from home."

"I'm tired of war and battles, of death and torture, of being tried in such a way that no truth will be accepted, and that only unwarranted accusations should be flung my way."

"Tell us; what happened next?" insisted Guillaume, seeing that Bernard was tired to the core, but continue with his story he must, for something needed to be revealed, something was of the matter and Bernard may be the very one to give the aid so sorely sought.

"The people of Acre insulted the Grand Master for no good reason," said Bernard. "They insisted that William de Beaujeu had no idea what he was talking about and that as soon as the payment of ransom was made, and the gates opened, that the Muslim's in the ranks of the siege army, as little as it was before them, would enact great vengeance and kill everyone within Acre. This they felt... knew, would happen once further support had arrived and their ranks swelled beyond all possible proportion."

"It sounds like the instigators of this tragedy felt guilty for what they had done, rallying for the support of others so that they wouldn't be tried for the eventual murder of innocents."

Bernard looked quizzically at Guillaume and Guillaume in turn saw the look and asked: "What is that look?"

"If my ears don't deceive me then I would swear that you hold no ill-feeling towards the Muslims in general," said Bernard.

"I'm a religious man but known to several Muslims that live not so far from me. They seem to be good people, but not all Muslims can be so-easily accepted. A vast majority are nothing more than evil-doers."

"It's how we saw it," said Bernard. "Often knights are compelled to rally to their Master's side, even when controversy is thick and flowing, but most of us, if not all, not only wished to stand beside de Beaujeu's decision, but believed in it."

Bernard eyed Guillaume as the French exchequer sat back down. Bernard continued. "In the end, all the people needed to do was to pay a single Venetian penny [penny sequin] The Sultan would have kept his word; he was a good man from everything that I learnt from the Templar Grand Master. Of course they would also be surrendering their homes, for the vacation of Acre would mean that they would not return; but can a life be sold for something as worthless as brick and mortar? The Master then preached to others, men and women alike, in churches around, in squares, in the light of God within the church known as the Church of Saint Cross. He did all he could to prevent catastrophe, to secure the safety of all within the city, but still they would not heed his great words of wisdom; and so the citizens of Acre turned upon him and called him a betrayer and that such a verdict of guilt should be punishable by death."

"You and the other knights stood beside your master, to encourage surrender, to give Acre over to the Muslims," accused Guillaume.

"We did as honourable men do, but it was for no good comfort, for the sultan died in his tent before hearing the verdict of the citizens of Acre," said Bernard.

"Yes," nodded Guillaume for the first time during the length of question and answer. "And then Kalaun's brother, Al Ashraf Khalil, took over the plight to have the citizens of Acre removed."

"That's right," said Bernard. "Ashraf was keener than Kalaun to see the seat of power transferred from one belief to the other. More siege engines were erected under the skilful expertise of engineers, and scimitars were sharpened by the professional touch of the blacksmith's anvil and hammer. The only good fortune was that winter was fast approaching and the advancement of Ashraf's army was postponed until the arrival of spring. It was only then that the true nature of their future was opened to them, for one and all to see, the fruits of their undoing coming to haunt them forever. The citizens were anxious, naturally enough, to find out what was to happen; what it was that the new sultan had upon his mind."

"And it's here that the weight of his answer fell upon all within the city," said Guillaume.

"Most of all, the Knights Templar," said Bernard. "A single Templar, a Hospitaller, and an Arab translator with a secretary, were cast upon a one-way trek, to approach the new sultan with many queries and the many possibilities for Acre's future. It came back to us by cowardly messenger, seated upon his horse and at the foot of the wall, not long after the good Hospitaller, and entourage, had gone to attend his errand, that they had all been jailed and then executed. This was the answer of peace; that no peace was possible between the Christians and the Muslims. The people of the city, so easy to sling accusations at the Grand Master, so quick to call him a coward, now gathered at his door to ask for savour.

"We desired surrender, but the people took it from the slate, and when the tables turned so did their mood. When a siege so seemingly weak but stubborn turns into a mass of siege engines and men with glistened points, so the citizenry lose all conviction, no bravery could be found amidst the many."

# Nine

Bernard sat at the table of their quarters, in the safety of the castle walls that surrounded them. Every now and again the sound of the siege reverberated through them; the walls of Acre targeted by catapults, from the ranks of the 160,000 strong, Muslim army under Ashraf.

"Did you hear of the Grand Master of the Teutonic Knights?" asked Edward as he took a drink from his tumbler, for there was a moment of solace where good men had the opportunity to fill their well, prior to taking post.

"Aye," acknowledged Matthew. "What could he be thinking, resigning in the face of the enemy, giving up all that he owed his Order, to then run like a coward, a scared dog?"

"It matters little," said Bernard. "The Teutonic are still here, have elected a new leader." He looked around the small table at the others that were seated. "All men doubt, all have sinned in one way or another."

"But vacating his responsibility," said Mark. "It's atrocious I say."

"The other knights of the Teutonic need our support and encouragement, not our words of criticism. It is we, the Templar, Hospitaller and Teutonic, that must come together in this time of need, and not only defend Acre, but the people that walk, and eat, and breath within it."

"I'll defend the miserable bastards," said Mark, "despite their reflections of cowardice, when they voiced accusations against William de Beaujeu in order to save their coin."

"We need to put all of this behind us," insisted Bernard. "The Hospitaller Knights have always been ready to stand beside us in times of war."

"And also quick to ridicule," added Edward.

"Nevertheless, we are all set for battle," said Bernard.

"Bernard, Mark!" yelled John as he rushed into the parlour where the others were drinking and talking.

"What is it, John?" questioned a concerned Bernard.

"The Genoese; they're loading their ships and preparing for sail, to leave the city to the security of us that remain behind," answered John.

"The defence of the city shouldn't be for us alone to attend," said Edward.

"Nevertheless," said Bernard. "We'll do all we can to protect Acre and all she holds."

"Do the Genoese hold that much spite towards the Venetians that they'd leave us in our time of need?" asked Matthew.

"It doesn't matter," said Bernard. "The city's still strong, surrounded by a good wall and supported by ten towers, as well as the Orders of Teutonic, Hospitaller and Templar."

"But the fighting will commence soon enough," said Matthew. "The preparatory has already commenced."

"This isn't the preparatory. It's simply a few machines ensuring they're within range. It will be a long time before any

Muslim sets foot within Acre;" said Bernard, "believe me. We're going to be in for a lot of sleepless nights before this siege turns ugly, which it will do before time."

"I saw many siege towers this morning," pointed out Mark.

"Aye, me too," said Edward.

"The wall and towers is only a temporary aid to our security," said John. "What'll we do when the walls are breached?"

"We'll do all we can," said Bernard, "and give aid to the citizens of this city, and to God. As for the Genoese, their untimely evacuation shall be remembered for what is it; cowardly and entirely unjust. As for now, well, we must return to duty."

# Ten

"And what did you do?" asked Guillaume.

"As an individual, or as part of the Order?"

"As a part of the defence," confirmed Guillaume.

"Helped maintain security upon the wall, as thin as it was. We only needed to maintain a picket within the towers. There would be warning enough when the attack finally came; we all thought this. An Army doesn't bring along such a vast number of catapults and then not put them to good use."

"How many catapults?" asked Guillaume.

"I should think there was at least sixty," replied Bernard. The three other men stopped what they were doing and looked up.

"That's ghastly," said Ricault Michaelensis. "I never read that in my reports so reverently placed upon my desk."

"It's the truth," said Bernard, looking from Ricault to Guillaume. "The sultan also commenced immediately to dig mines beneath the city walls in the hope to have them come crashing down when the supports to each mine were set on fire. Something needed to be done."

"And what did you do?" asked Guillaume.

"The very first volleys of the attack came on the sixth day of April, raining down upon the walls and towers like nothing I'd ever seen before. They continued without rest for forty days and forty nights, one after the other, ceaseless in their uncaring way, bringing devastation and depression, and much regret too."

"Regret?" asked Guillaume, looking for a better explanation; a learned man seeking clearer facts.

"The regret felt by those that had caused this great upset at the very beginning, the raucous that was ravaging the city: regret as to the offence off-handed to the Muslims by the few of the city some time past, those that thought nothing in bringing our relationship with Kalaun to an end by chastising and murdering Muslim citizens, and whether done so deliberately or not matters little. Here, I say, that thoughtless actions breed malignant ends; mindless actions are clouded by poor sense," said Bernard.

He continued. "Fire, stone and arrows filled the sky. I knew of one knight in particular, so honourable in all that he carried out, being filled with much grief. It was when the lance that he carried was consumed by dozens of notches created by arrows; appearing so vast upon his weapon in the time it takes a man to draw a single breath. The air was so thick with missiles that it simply can't be put into words."

"But you remained in place?" prodded Guillaume, becoming acquainted with Bernard and his efforts.

"There's not much that can be done against an army of over six hundred thousand."

"Six... you said that there were one hundred and sixty thousand," said Guillaume.

"In the ranks, the front ranks, those standing ready to carry out their foreseen justice, prior to the siege turning nasty: give or take a few," said Bernard. "The true size of the army was divided into companies. There was much rest and relaxation for those before the wall. Ashraf Khalil had a detachment of one hundred thousand or more, simply to attend to the resupply duties. It seemed that for every soldier we killed, two would take his place."

"And still you stood upon the wall, warding off the devil, preventing him from entering the city, fighting him from a wall so solidly built," said Guillaume.

"Yes and no," said Bernard. "The Knights Templar defends well, I grant you that, but we were used to being the attacker, not the defender, and so we set upon taking the war to them."

"Take the war to them!" Guillaume was excited by this, and needed to learn more. "How did you do that?" asked Guillaume.

"You saw the largest scar upon my back, the length of it," said Bernard. "That one was not from a torturer, but from a scimitar. I was lucky to get away with my life intact."

# Eleven

Bernard sat upon his mount as the others gathered around, many horses coming under the command of the knights that rode them. They were three hundred men awaiting their opportunity to attack the Muslim camp and bring much despair upon it, the afternoon having drawn to a close, with the evening in full spread before them.

Bernard could see all of his friends around him, but most of all he saw Edward and Matthew.

There was a little cloud cover above, but not too much, and the moon was nowhere to be seen; nevertheless, the night was darker than they had hoped for.

The Knights Templar held onto their reigns, all three hundred prepared and ready for the gates of St. Lazarus to be opened, and as they were pulled open the thunderous noise of three hundred war horses filled the air.

Across the open ground they pressed, forever on towards the tents of their enemy which they knew existed, but the dark of the night was against them as it was their Muslim counterparts. The night, having been considered a friend on this foray into battle, soon turned against them all.

The tents were reached, the mass of ropes lying about, pulled taunt or loose, got tangled up with the horses legs, and one after the other the knights and the horses alike fell to the ground; legs broken, necks broken, spirits broken. The lights of the camp were not enough to pave their way but enough to fight in.

The Muslims erupted from the tents and the scimitar was soon connecting with the sword of the knight, as the Templar commenced their fight against the Muslim scum. The surprise attack was no longer a surprise, the advantage of the night and general assault had now turned against the Order. But for the most part the Muslims had been woken from slumber and as such were not owners of full faculty, hence easier to kill.

Melee was engaged thick and fast, much blood being spilled, many screams of death filling the breaches of the air around, amidst the neighing of horses: there was nothing worse than a dying horse, one so eager to please, one that had served its rider so well, to be left dying like a scoundrel dog: except that of a dying comrade.

One after the other, brave men fell to the blood-soaked desert mat and Bernard felt the stinging of a scimitar blade upon his back, being assailed by three men, two of which were to his front.

He could only make out the semblance of the men's shapes as they continued the fight and suddenly he killed two with a single swinging motion of his weapon of war, its ballet seeing to it that he could now concentrate on the scimitar-wielding man to his rear.

Suddenly, from out of nowhere, a rescuer came into view, seated high upon the only horse standing on four legs.

"Bernard! Bernard," yelled Edward as loudly as he could,

trying with all his effort to snatch his friend out of his one-track mind, where the ravenous battle had taken hold of all his senses. Unknown to himself, he was fighting like a madman, a man with superpower, out of control, of single mind and purpose.

"Bernard; up here my friend," yelled Edward once more. Bernard shook the raging battle from his mind and looked up to the seated form of the Templar upon his horse.

Bernard was hence pulled to the relative safety upon the saddle by his friend Edward, and together they were sprinted back towards the safety of the walls.

# Twelve

"You turned your back and then ran, to save your own neck," accused Guillaume, or seemingly so; but that was not his intention.

"Would you have done any difference? I could have died then and there, but I lived to fight a better battle," said Bernard. "Would it change your opinion to consider, for just a moment, that I was not in control of the horse I was riding upon, that it was my friend, Edward, who had hold of the reigns?"

"Would it have made a difference if you held them?" asked Guillaume.

Bernard felt as though he couldn't lie. "Probably not; but in the heat of battle... I do not know?"

Guillaume could see that he had overstepped the bounds of his duty to his country and that he was being unfair to Bernard.

"I didn't mean it to sound as though I was accusing you," said Guillaume, in his first acknowledgement that Bernard was right to do as he had done. "I meant only—"

"...Meant only to accuse or assume... it doesn't matter. What matters is that Edward gave his life for me," said Bernard, noticing the stares of the men around him. "Yes, indeed; Edward was pierced by many arrows, arrows stuck in his front and a few from behind having hit him in the shoulder, having missed me by mere whiskers. He died later that night. It wasn't until we were safely back behind the walls of Acre, along with five other men, all of whom had been saved from death, that we'd heard of the massacre we'd been subjected to. It was very dark that night, where only a little illumination could be gained from a few camp fires and burning torches amidst the Muslim camp."

"Your position within the walls must have been drastically affected by the loss of so many men and horses?" said Guillaume.

"The loss of manpower was devastating, but some of the horses we got back," said Bernard. "The enemy had them placed upon the catapults and they were flung over the walls, usually in pieces: a head here, a few legs there; even some whole in body though limbless, as though common rocks; the carcasses would burst open on contact with the ground... it was terrible to see the horror on the faces of the citizens and their children."

"Better a horse than a man," said Guillaume.

"Oh, Templar heads were also delivered to us, sailing through the air and landing behind the walls, delivering further calamity and poor feeling amongst the growing desperation."

"It must have been hard to live down; this defeat," said Guillaume.

"The Hospitallers were quite accommodating when it came to accusations, but then again they fared no better. On a similar night they too pushed on into the night, to show us how such an attack should have been carried out, but the enemy lit brush fires on hearing the sound of the hooves crashing across the open ground and the assault was called off: the heathen scum had learnt a lesson from the past. So where lies the heroism? We, the Knights Templar, were massacred till only a handful returned, and the Hospitaller; they returned fully stocked. And so before you sling accusations of cowardice and surrender to fall upon the shoulder of the Knights Templar, maybe you should consider what it was that the Teutonic and Hospitaller did during the defence. Our master did all he could to give aid to the people; The Grand Master of the Teutonic resigned and the Hospitaller called off an assault immediately on seeing a little flame upon the horizon. If you ask me, it's the Knights Templar that deserves the reward of congratulations."

"If the destruction and calamity was as bad as you say... surely it would have worked better to bring the people together," said Guillaume.

"On the contrary, they continued to hate and to loath, even with the host of thousands slinging rock and horse into our domain. Oh, yes; Acre fell, rather too easily," admitted Bernard and then gave good reason. "The walls grew weaker by the day; day after day the cracks grew larger in the masonry, volley after volley delivering much hatred and catastrophe; the catapults were ceaseless in their deliverance of vengeance, a vengeance which had manifested itself into a battle to end all battles. By May the sixteenth one of the ten towers fell to the ground and a gaping hole suddenly appeared within the defence. The enemy swarmed in like ants over the carcass of an insect. Much valuable ground was lost, ground that could not be afforded. The walls and towers bound the city and now it was falling. The sultan ordered a full attack to take place, and from all sides they attacked simultaneously, the crazed Muslim invaders penetrating from all sides. When the first of the sultan's army set foot into Acre, the citizens continued to fight and condemn. One party of men would run away to leave the defence of a particular sector to another, wiping their hands clean of the responsibility. Whilst the Muslim scum ravaged the city and castles within, the men and women would rally to their own flag and quarter, leaving the desperate to fend for themselves, to try and ward off the enemy from entering their castle or palace. It didn't take long, due to the insanity and ill-feeling amongst them all, to see the Muslim invaders take precious hold of castles and palaces, storming the breaches they'd secured, killing those within. Many slaves were taken, many women raped, many children butchered for no good reason. The people of Acre were mostly mad, never lifting a finger to help another, but thinking only of themselves. This is why Acre fell, because of the peasant army of thousands, because of the mercenary that had been sent to the city to protect it; but mainly because citizens would only protect their own quarter, their own grounds, that little piece of Acre which was partitioned just for them. They say a mans' home is his castle, but here we see that the castle is his home. They were rallying to their own cause, their own flag, their own banner, instead of coming together and fighting as one. They were like a disease, spreading from one quarter to another, people turning into savage monsters, promoting their own downfall due to greed and cowardice. All over the face of Acre did the enemy storm this palace and that, taking what they wanted, commencing with the pillage of all that was of Christian value."

Guillaume and the others were drawn to every word that Bernard spoke, enthralled by what had taken place, a first-hand account as to the true magnitude of the tragedy.

"It was at this time that the Orders within Acre saw the true light, saw it all for themselves, that the only way to survive the pestilence of slaughter swallowing the community at large was to defend what was its own. We did as the others had done," said Bernard. "The Templar, Hospitaller and Teutonic fought hard against the Saracens, fought with sword, tooth and nail, but in their own quarters. And the fighting continued on and on without relent until, together with their followers, every single Teutonic Knight in Acre was dead, their castle swallowed up by the enemy as they swarmed over the breaches like locusts. There was no saving them. They died, each and every one of them, at the same time, rushing into the mass of scimitar-wielding scum as they pressed forward their attack."

# *Thirteen*

"It was at around this time that the assault upon the city then turned upon us, the Knights Templar. Our Grand Master, de Beaujeu, was killed, skewered by an arrow as thousands filled the sky, too-vast-a-number to be contemplated. Over the walls the arrows flew without concern for where they landed and as our master reached upwards with his sword in his hand he was hit by a missile," Bernard looked from one to the other in seeming astonishment. "The arrow found a small partition in the armour, where the master was unprotected, and... he was killed... but not straight away."

"I heard it was a javelin," said Guillaume.

"It matters not!" spat Bernard. "He was courageous to the end. From all around we knights urged him to stay and help with the fighting; begged of him. But he couldn't do any more, even though he wished to continue with the fight. Before the sun disappeared that day he was dead, killed by the fatal wound he had received."

"We heard that the Master was acting more like a coward," said Guillaume.

"No, it's not true," insisted Bernard. "Someone with such a huge responsibility doesn't give in so easily. Our master was filled with so many years of good service that courage spilled from within. He was one of the strongest men it was my honour to have served under."

"What happened next?"

"It was then that the Hospitaller quarter was breached by many Muslims and they stormed the breach in the wall, bringing the battle into their very midst, slaughter upon slaughter filling the air... you could hear it upon the wind, the metal upon metal, sword clashing with scimitar and shield against buckler," said Bernard, seeing it with his own eyes as he spoke the words so dreadful.

He continued. "The Saint Anthony gate was then opened by the enemy from within, and the enemy on the outside stormed through. The Hospitaller Grand Master was then wounded... I'm not sure how. I heard later that he wished to fight on, insisted that he remain with the others of his Order, but he was forcibly removed from contact, carried away to safety and dispatched from Acre via one of their many boats at sea."

"Hard it is, to believe the words passed on by those that were amidst a battle, for their memory can be so conflicting, more so by their immediate actions than anything else" said Guillaume.

"You question his heroism," stated Bernard. "If his spirit should hear you condemn him that way then he shall fall upon you before the night is out. Don't forget the fallen, how they fought to save the face of Christian belief."

"You're right," said Guillaume, "of course. I've seen a report from John de Villiers, describing in much detail the final hours of the defence. But nevertheless, it's still tainted with the exaggeration of battle noise and excitement."

"Death is not exciting," insisted Bernard, "it's heinous."

"But still you fight on, from one year to the next you fight and fight and fight."

"I am a soldier, where being cast from a peasant or a Knights Templar matters little; I am who I am."

"Indeed, you are that," said Guillaume.

"And what did you read in this report of yours?" asked Bernard.

"That the enemy was so vast in number that there was absolutely no way anyone could count them; that they swarmed over the dead like a plague... a sea of black mist voicing its hatred against a common cause," said Guillaume. "It was recorded that the Saracens were driven back three times, prevented from entering at the expense of the blood of good Christian men."

"Women and children were slaughtered too," added Bernard. Said Guillaume, as though not hearing: "The marshal of the Order, Brother Matthew de Clement, was also killed that day, and bestowed upon him was much praise and comradeship. And many fled the battle, seeing that the fight could not be won."

"Not all fled the scene, to retreat to the sea," said Bernard. "Not everyone within Acre was so quick to give up her defence. Many brave souls decided to remain behind, to continue the fight, to buy time for those that had reached the security of the galleys that awaited them. We didn't all flee," finished an exhausted Bernard.

"No? And what do you know of this, of the slaughter that occurred on the  inside of the Hospitaller grounds?" asked Guillaume.

"Several of their Order came into our arms, having been rescued by a handful," said Bernard.

"And were you a part of this 'handful'?" queried Guillaume.

"No, not I; but others I knew," admitted Bernard. "When they fell into our care I was swallowed by emotion."

# *Fourteen*

The days of fighting in Acre continued on and one, more so for the Hospitaller than anyone else, for the Saracens had concentrated their assault upon that quarter of the city.

A Hospitaller named Martin was fighting side by side with his brothers when the last of the breaches was forced open, a cascade of snarling men in turbans racing to the glory of gold and slaves.

Martin looked around him and with great sharpness felt the dread he thought he'd never have to feel. The walls were growing thick with the enemy and soon after the initial positions upon the wall fell, so did the others around them.

"Flee, flee!" came a voice from the rear.

"Ahhh.... run away," came another, muffled by the fact that his back was turned upon Martin as the man ran in the opposite direction, for the safety that might be offered by the sea.

"No!" yelled Martin. "We have to stay, remain in place; the Lord will give you strength if only you should look for it."

Suddenly a lance fell from heaven and struck Martin in the right shoulder, his sword arm. There was to be no further fighting for him.

"Martin, are you alright," came the reasonably calm question from a brother in arms.

Martin looked up into the man's eyes. "Yes, Peter," he said. "I'll survive this day."

"But not for long, not unless we gather speed this instant," said Peter. "Come, old friend, let's get you to your feet and out of here."

Martin stood and looked Peter forcibly in the eye. "We can't depart, we can't leave this city. Our duty is not done."

"It's finished, Martin," insisted Peter. "There's nothing...." he turned suddenly and with his sword still in his master hand did parry the strong blow of a scimitar and then skewer the man who had tried his luck in killing two men with a single slash. "We have to leave, the city has fallen."

"The Knights Templar," urged Martin. "They still stand, and whilst hope still remains so does the courage of men."

"It's too far."

"Don't let fear stop you, Peter."

Peter paused for a moment. "It's words like that that'll lose you your friends someday," said Peter.

"Come, old friend, get me to the Templar castle."

# *Fifteen*

Martin looked up into Bernard's eyes as he laid there. "That's how it was," he said. "But now... you must get me to my feet so that I can get used to walking once more."

"You're still weak," said Bernard, concerned for the well-being of the Hospitaller. "You're a brave man, Martin; both you and Peter have more courage than most."

"Where is Peter?" asked Martin.

"He was struck by an arrow as you both came through our sally port," replied Bernard, his heart sinking.

"He was the bravest, wishing to see me delivered here this day," said Martin. "He fought and killed over a dozen men on our way here; me, a great weight and burden... I pressed him to get me here so that I could continue with my sworn duty."

"And there's plenty of duty to be performed," added Bernard. "You'll be sick to death of seeing the red cross upon our white tunic before your time is done."

"How does the defence hold?" asked Martin.

"Very well, but for how long, no one knows," replied Bernard. "As for now, I must be off. I have duties of my own to perform."

"Where is your chapel?"

"Just around the corner, after you exit this building," answered Bernard.

"I'll make my way there shortly, and give praise to all of those that have fallen or who have fled," said Martin. "There are many sergeants, mercenaries and crusaders, not to mention the scores of poor lads and other civilians that have perished this day. The wounded and sick were carried away to safety within the boats by strong men of heart, by the household boys and sergeants alike. There was no danger for them, just a duty to perform."

"We all have our duty," agreed Bernard.

"I have been lucky to escape, to fight again in the arms of comradeship as that bestowed upon me, by men like you, Bernard."

"I have to go now," said Bernard. "I wish you luck."

# Sixteen

"And that was the last I saw of Martin," said Bernard.

"You speak of much valour," said Guillaume.

"It was everywhere you looked. Every soldier, sailor and candlestick maker; every single soul had a heart of courage."

"But what about those that fled? The nobles, the leader of the Swiss, Otto de Grandson, and the English army under his banner being loaded onto Venetian vessels and fleeing like scared rabbits; the citizens, so many there were, all fleeing to Cyprus; what about their souls?"

"I speak of those loyal to the cause, those of Christian faith," answered Bernard. "I can't speak for those that were conceited and full of greed."

"And what next, what of the Templar defence?" asked Guillaume.

"It stood strong, all two hundred of us that remained, except..."

"Yes," urged Guillaume, eager to hear what was to come after such a mystifying pause.

"There was one man, a Knights Templar, who showed all his true colours," started Bernard. "Roger de Flor commandeered a Templar galley. He could see the city was falling; there was no doubt in that. He offered all manner of men and women a safe passage away from Acre, so long as they could afford such passage. Anyone with the financial support for such a venture could approach and pay a mighty sum in order to be given a place upon his galley for the voyage to safer quarters. And many people took up the offer."

"One man in many," said Guillaume. "That's not bad odds."

"You surprise me, Guillaume," said Bernard. "You seem to be taking my side."

"I'm a just man," answered Guillaume. "I'm sure he had his reasons to depart; maybe not as good a reason as those that stayed, but nevertheless."

"He won't sup in heaven," replied Bernard. "Not that I care what happens to him. But you do have to have an appreciation for the situation."

"Tell me," insisted Guillaume. Bernard looked around the table at all those present, each silent and waiting with bated breath to hear more on the fall of Acre.

"The air continued to be filled with arrows and then as the city began to burn more feverishly than before, the hail of missiles in the air seemed to abate. The smoke was so thick and widespread that it was impossible to see from one castle or palace to another. Only when the Saracens were upon their defences did anyone know that they were in danger of being breached. All across Acre the castles, palaces and other defences were attacked; many at the same time; and other stations were sacked once another had been taken. It was only then that the citizens threw aside their citizenship and other prejudices to fight side by side with others of the city: only now did they fight as citizens of Acre as opposed to citizens of their quarter. The people came together then, to help one another, something they should have done many weeks before," said Bernard.

Sorrow filled Bernard's eyes. "It was too late now to make amends. Fire consumed buildings, filled the air with smoke, and choked all of those around, both Christian and Muslim alike. But fire wasn't the only thing against us all. The land around was so dry, as dry as a dog's bone left to the conditions of weather and time, so hot and dry that it drank the spilt blood of men, women, and children, as fast as it flowed from their wounds. Water; so scarce it was, and yet the sea was as rough as you'd ever seen it. At first it was calm, but no sooner did the galleys and other boats fill with those wishing to escape and God answered with all the might of his vengeance. God looked unfavourably upon the deserters. A storm came out from nowhere. Many thousands were drowned: they were running scared from a Christian city; a sinking city; but it was God's city."

"And many thousands escaped," said Guillaume. "Well in excess of one hundred thousand made it to Cyprus and beyond. I know this to be true."

"Which just goes to show you how many cowards were truly bred in the city of Acre," said Bernard. "Acre's defences had been left to those of the three Orders; and the few that were courageous enough to stand by their side."

"They paid the price," said Guillaume. "But you, you stayed and fought; and now... you are testament to the sin of those that fled."

"It's only testament if it is believed," said Bernard as he looked deep into Guillaume's eyes.

"Which is the duty of this small... assembly, to prove or disprove," replied Guillaume. "Are you speaking the whole truth, and nothing but?"

"I am," answered Bernard, and the truth of it all could be clearly seen in his eyes.

"Will you please continue with your story?" insisted an intrigued man, the one known as Ricault Michaelensis.

"Yes," said Bernard, "that will be an honour in itself, to allow the good men that stayed to fight the heathen Saracens acknowledgement for their sacrifice and great courage," and then he paused for a moment.

"I know, only from hearsay, of course, that almost five hundred fair maidens, ladies, and daughters to princes and kings, fled to the shoreline, to hand over their jewels and other embellishments to captains, the price for a ticket away from death's door," said Bernard.

"Gold and all manner of precious stone filled the pockets of the men upon their decks as the rich boarded their vessels of the sea. They were so desperate, each and every one of them. A friend of my, one I have spoken of earlier, came and said to me, after assisting some of them to safety, that the women of high status were selling themselves, giving themselves up as wives to hungry sex-crazed men, giving a promise to wed with them if only they could be taken far away from Acre."

"I can easily believe it," said Guillaume. "I've heard of women, being both of noble status or a common damsel, selling themselves off for the gift of life," said Guillaume. "But can anyone blame them; such mischievous creatures of God they are. And what of the city; tell me more?"

"People were slain," said Bernard. "The Saracens were making their way through the city, from castle to castle, from palace to palace, from church to church, killing most they came into contact with. There was much gold to be had in the form of slaves, but the old and the young, those too old to perform good duty, and those still suckling at their mothers' breast, were killed on the spot. They trampled here and there, over the fallen, over the corpses that littered the ground. There wasn't a place in the entire city where the ground could be seen for the dead that covered it. The dead were the cobbles; the dead were the roads and the paths. The dead received no respect for what they once were. Men, women, and children, were shackled and taken away, to serve as slaves."

"How many did you protect in the end?" asked Guillaume. "How many came to you for protection?"

"There were over seven thousand that came to us," said Bernard, and he saw Johannes Blanke gasp slightly in disbelief. "It's true. We were but two hundred Templars fighting to protect the lives of over seven thousand. They came to us in droves, lucky to make it to within our walls. The inner city was lost but our castle still stood strong. Every single one of us that remained did vow to remain behind and protect those that feared for their lives, those that were too poor to buy a ticket away from hell, or too ugly in the eyes of sailors to be taken as a wife. Those with children were inevitably left to us for protection, discarded like common garbage."

"How, in God's name, did you feed them?" asked Guillaume.

"A good question indeed, one that the Sultan had obviously not considered, for he could have waited for us to perish, there in front of his very eyes, but instead he sent to us an envoy."

"So; what happened next?" asked Ricault.

"After five days of hard fighting, and more at siege, the Sultan realised that there was little he could do to unseat us. He proposed to spare the lives of all the women and the children, to let us all depart the castle with our weapons and all we could carry. It was an offer too good to be refused. Were we to allow seven thousands to be killed by the scimitar, or become victorious and see them all saved? It was easy to answer."

"You fell for his treachery," said Guillaume, accusingly.

"I am not an authority, I am but a soldier; a crusader sworn to serve the Lord and peasants alike."

"That could be considered blasphemous," said Guillaume.

"You're probably right. All men are seen as equals through the eyes of the Lord. No one is above the Lord, but all are the same," said Bernard. "And you wouldn't be so quick to accuse me if you were to see the fright displaced upon the faces of those we protected. It is true, we were stationed in a castle, in the strongest part of the city, which happened to look over the sea. We were surrounded on all sides by good walls, but also the enemy in their thousands... tens of thousands. Acre had been practically burnt to the ground and all that remained within the city's walls was the Templar castle. But we were a mischievous bunch of men and so, seeing the Saracens mining beneath the grounds around us, did mine ourselves, this commenced many weeks prior, and we toppled a tower upon them, killing them where they hid, away from the fire and smoke, hidden from view and out of harm's way. You must remember that we had an extensive system of underground tunnels and so mining was much easier for us to establish. The Saracens must have suffered terribly, buried beneath the ground in their tunnels of refuge."

"So it was in the face of great defeat that the Sultan offered his gift," stated Guillaume.

"And the gift was accepted," said Bernard.

# *Seventeen*

Bernard continued with his story. "And as we all commenced to depart the castle the Muslim scum began to molester the women and young boys as quick as they were able to hoist the banner of the Sultan. We were utterly outraged by the acts we saw before us, outraged that the women looking to us for protection should be treated in such a way, and so we took matters into hand. Our commander, Peter de Severy, gave the order and we quickly barred the castle doors and drew our weapons from their sheaths, slaughtering all the Saracen scum we could find within, and once again the Beauseant was hoisted to fly high and mighty over the crowd of enemy as they watched on. It was then and there that we condemn ourselves to death."

"But you live," said Guillaume.

"I swore to protect the innocent, as every Templar before me has done," said Bernard. "Our treasurer, Tibauld de Gaudin, loaded what he could of the treasure we had and took with him as many women and children as possible. He then set sail for Sidon and safety. The very next day, as the sun peeked over the horizon, the Sultan sent another envoy and vowed to punish those Saracen men that had committed crimes against us, they being guilty and acting in poor fashion, and he gave his apologies for it. De Severy took kindly to these words and with a handful of knights decided to meet with the Sultan once more, and no sooner had he stepped through the doors of the castle... they were all butchered, beheaded in front of those watching from the walls."

Bernard could see that he had everyone's attention. "There was to be no compromise of any description. And so the mining commenced again and within time the walls of our castle were brought crumbling down, upon us and the enemy alike. We took up our arms and rushed the Saracen scum, and many died over the coming hours. And in likeness of the good that we bestowed upon those that we protected came the order to see to it that as many women and children should be saved as possible, and so a retreat was commenced to the shore and a few managed to escape."

"And so you retreated as did many others?" said Guillaume.

"No, I lead the way to victory and God's arms by attacking the enemy, buying time for the women and children to make their escape," said Bernard. "But I was captured alive, and with the kindness bestowed within some of the good citizens of Acre a ransom was arranged for me and several children to be saved from the scars of humility. I was once more saved."

"And so Acre is lost," said Guillaume. "I see now the truth, all that has been recorded, all that has been said. The Knights Templar were the last to depart Acre, be they dead or alive."

"We did all we could do," said Bernard, "and so yes, we were the last in Acre, the last to die, the last to withdraw for the good of the few women and children that could be saved, and yet, for all our good action comes the accusations from the king of

France."

Bernard then drew upon a comparison. "There is more greed in this man than all the Saracen put together, for he alone has seen to it that the Knights Templar have been wiped from the face of the earth."

"You served gallantly," said Guillaume.

"And for what?" said Bernard. "Didn't the pope himself give advice to us poor wretched souls, who spend our days, weeks and years, protecting pilgrims of many cast, that a promise of benefits both religious and secular would be reaped by those who took part in the crusades and battles against the Mohammedans. This was the way in which the Church fostered the crusades? As a warrior myself, a man of respect for the God I love, I was to enjoy forgiveness of all my past sins, of which there are so few that I can hardly recall a single one. If I was to die fighting for my faith I was to be assured an immediate entrance to the joys of Paradise, freed by the Church from paying interest on debts; of which I have none. And I was to be provided assistance by lawful avenue to have excommunicated anyone who should dare to molest my wife, child, or property; none of which is possessed by me; for I serve no one but God Himself."

"Yes indeed," agreed Guillaume. "But the pope is dead now and only the king lives."

"Why is it that the French king is so... thought provokingly and heinously real, through character of deliverance, dispelled the Templar when they did so much for Europe?" asked Bernard before continuing. "If it wasn't for the men of the crusades then the commerce of the country would be well short of how it stands at present. I, and men like me, have created a constant demand for transportation of men and supplies by encouraging the building of ships and allowing for the promotion and marketing of the wares of the East into the West. Products of Mosul, Cairo, Damascus, and Alexandria, just to name a few, have found their way into seaports right across the Mediterranean and into cities of Germany, France, Spain and Portugal; once again, just to name a few. Never before has this grand world of ours seen the elegance of the orient close up, where prying eyes and fingertips could come into contact with such a vast array of beauty and elegance, such as the silks, tapestries, precious stones, perfumes, spices, pearls, and ivory, so lavish in all their power that they are the vestibules to a good man's heart and mind, not to mention that of a woman. Great wealth and reputation has been attained through the blood of men like me, through the fostering needs of the crusaders."

"But wealth shouldn't be reason alone to consider your position as being justified," said Guillaume. "There is more to life than wealth and yet the Templars seemed quite content to save what they could of their treasure, seeing to it that Peter de Severy, before becoming the new Grand Master, did depart Acre with all that he could carry. This, you understand, is not everyone's point of view, but needs to be aired."

"Especially for you, the French Exchequer," said Bernard. "We have helped stem feudalism in such a way that it is good, for all involved, in particular those of high position. Thousands upon thousands of knights and barons have mortgaged their lands and other property in order to serve, and where rich men of position have died for the cause of war with the unworthy, their estates have been reverted in ownership to fall within the grasp of the crown. There is no more private warfare between holders of grand estates, no feudal conflict to speak of, and correspondingly the growth of the royal authority has received great encouragement through such actions of heroism. It is to the sacrifice of many that the prominence of kings and countries can be attested. The very enrichment of civilization can be seen through the artefacts on display across Europe, the spoils of the East helping to develop various arts, inventions, and the ways of manufacture. Where's the greed in that; how do men like me prosper from such wealth?"

Guillaume looked to Johannes Blanke who handed him a stare. Johannes then spoke. "The script of those within the Order was created in order to serve and protect the pilgrims, and others like them that undertook the pilgrimage, that suffering, long trek, from country to country, over many lands of sovereign sway and judgement. It would seem, justifiably enough to say, that such an Order already existed; the Knights Hospitaller were already suited to provide aid to those seeking redemption from sins performed in the sight of the Lord: from God. So shouldn't it be said that the Knights Templar was more interested in protecting their own wealth?"

"To protect their wealth; or is it that they were protecting something more?" said Bernard.

"And there we have it," said Guillaume, as though successful in the charade, having succeeded in bringing out into the open something of importance. "Are you saying they were formed to protect something from the ever-lasting greed of man, something of Holy importance?"

"I believe that no more than I believe your accusations of our interest in wealth and status, but it's there for you to compare, to see for yourself how accusation can go too far," said Bernard. "There seems to be a lot of jealousy amongst the crowns of Europe, of the Templar's wealth and steadfastness. Many wanted to see them dethroned of their position within society and the pages of history, to have them seen as something evil and untoward, where slanderous rumours spread like a common disease of secret rituals and of Templar's worshipping the devil."

"Nevertheless," said Guillaume, "such a position held by your Order worked well towards a financial boom for you all."

"And for the crown," stated Bernard. "They were learned men, even if transcended from peasant, all of the Templars, who had sworn to protect pilgrims of all religions and nationality as they travelled across flourishing and barren lands to pay homage to their God, in more cases than not so that they could receive forgiveness for sins committed. They had minds to rival others, understanding the politics of the time, situation, and location, as well as be financially secure and mature, being good traders and backed up by their brothers in arms. Just because they were intelligent enough to help fund their own ventures should be no reason to sling accusations."

"Let's go back, just a moment," said Guillaume, "to your own words; 'or is it that they were protecting something more'. Some have said that in their trust; in your trust; was cast the secrets held at bay from the community at large, which also included those of the cloth, preserving vast amounts of sacred knowledge and artefact, be it information on the Temple of Solomon or the

Great Pyramid and Atlantis; or the location of the Holy Grail, Ark of the Covenant, or Cross of Christ. For instance, found in Chartres Cathedral is the image of the quest for the Holy Grail."

# Eighteen

Bernard felt then that Guillaume was after something sounder, something that he knew nothing about.

"The meaning of the short phrase, on occasion heard, 'protection of something so sacred and important', is shunned by the Hospitaller," said Bernard in reply, "an Order you seem to be so fond of; so go speak with them. It is the Hospitaller who wished to know what-it-was-all-about, but they were to be disappointed, as was the inquisition."

"Can you blame anyone for wanting to know the truth of it all?" said Guillaume. "The ranks of the Knights Templar grew rapidly, a true enough indication of something unsavoury going on."

"I disagree wholeheartedly," said Bernard. "On the contrary to what you say, when noblemen joined our ranks they relinquished their entire property and the revenues from such were used to purchase weapons, war-horses, armour and other military supplies, and most of the order took vows of poverty, chastity, and obedience. We served the Lord and the people equally; the Lord with service and the people with protection. Is it no surprise, then, how the Templar wealth grew so strong and vast?"

"But the Knights Templar, as you must admit, were seen to own over nine thousand manors and castles right across the face of Europe, the revenues from each supporting the largest banking system in the Christian world," said Guillaume. "This shouldn't be forgotten."

"And there too, is another answer for you; to which I have no doubt, that you are already aware," said Bernard.

"And that is?"

"That King Philip convinced Pope Clement that the Templar were not the bold supporters of their Holy faith but the devils in disguise, looking to destroy the religion," replied Bernard. "King Philip of France wanted nothing more than for them all to be persecuted because of their financial and political power. It was then that the pope gave orders for an inquisition to begin, and right across France the Templar were arrested."

"But many fled, including the naval force which was anchored in La Rochelle."

"Can you blame them? All of those arrested were tried and found guilty; it would have been no different for those anchored by the shores of La Rochelle," defended Bernard.

"Let us pause," said Guillaume, "just for a moment. Have a drink of water, Bernard; quench your thirst."

Bernard took a drink and leaned back a little, looking again into the eyes of all those seated around him, each taking notes or reading them.

"My job today," commenced Guillaume, "is not to find you guilty... guilty; no. I am simply here to find out more about you, Bernard, to get down to the truth of your life."

"And why should my life be so important?"

"You are on the brink as going down as the man who killed the pope," said Guillaume "None of us here believes in your guilt, but belief isn't enough."

"Are you scared that history shall see it that a Templar killed the pope? Or is it the king that's afraid of giving them the power he wished them to be deprived of?"

"When your master was burnt as the stake he gave notice that the pope and the king would fall."

"And the king is concerned for his safety?"

"Shouldn't he be?" asked Guillaume.

"I guess there must be many men around hoping to get their grubby little hands around the king's throat. Including the French Exchequer," said Bernard, receiving a sudden stare from them all.

"No one is without good reason," said Guillaume. "But you are seen as a threat where I am not."

"Let's move on to the trial in Cyprus," said Imbert. "Maybe a change of note will give you some small satisfaction."

"Maybe," said Bernard. "But then again, maybe you have hidden agendas."

"Let's begin," said Guillaume. "One hundred and Twenty six questions were asked of witnesses to the Templars' behaviour. Men like James of Plany; Rupen of Montfort; and Percival, Lord of Mar. There was a story that the Knights Templar were offered freedom by the Egyptian Sultan if they would deny their God. In what would seem to be true Templar fashion, as in accordance with what you have been saying this day, they refused to deny the Christian faith. Each and every knight captured was willing to be put to death rather than deny their God; to be decapitated as opposed to denying Jesus Christ, their savour. They were then refused access to food and water and their gaolers locked them away to perish as they did. Such strength in men only goes to prove that the Knights Templar would not go against all that they believed; but the inquisition saw to it that many confessed."

"In the face of torture," said Bernard.

"Yes," agreed Guillaume. "In the face of torture, just as you, yourself, have admitted to killing the pope: in the face of torture."

"Death by starvation is easier to handle," said Bernard.

"How do you know?"

"It's a guess... I've been tortured in the past; there is no room for dying with dignity when tortured to death, to be seen screaming out denials."

"Others, too, have sworn to the heroism of knights," continued Guillaume. "Take for example that of Thomas, Lord of Pingueno. He said that he saw many knights decapitated as they didn't wish to deny their Lord."

"A quick death is a good death when on the battlefield," said Bernard. "It's very merciful."

"Balian, Lord of Montgisard; Marshal of Cyprus, Ayme of Osilliers; and others like them, all swear that the Templars are noble warriors and uphold their vows of chastity and obedience; and above all, that they possessed no idols. Even bishops have said that the Knights Templar believed in the sacraments of the altar and of the church. It seems to me, therefore, in the face of so many witnesses, all of which can be trusted, that you, as an Order, are incapable of blasphemous and sacrilegious acts."

"Thank you," said Bernard. "It seems that your task here is

done."

"On the contrary, I still have much I wish to discuss."

"I'm growing tired," said Bernard. "It's not easy being locked away in a dungeon with little to no food. The water helps, but doesn't serve to take away my hunger."

"I have no food," said Guillaume, "and nor am I about to disrupt this meeting of ours whilst we have done so well. We'll continue until we're done, and then, I give you my word upon it, you can have all you wish to eat."

"Very well," said Bernard. "Let the water do its trick and let's get the questioning over with."

"Thank you," said Guillaume as he prepared himself for the task of asking more questions.

# Nineteen

"John Balliol was crowned king of Scotland at Scone in 1292," said Guillaume.

"What does this have to do with the pope?" asked Bernard.

"It is necessary," said Guillaume.

"Very well."

"He was crowned in 1292 and in April of 1296 he renounced his homage to Edward, king of England. King Edward then invaded Scotland and sacked Berwick. The Battle of Dunbar then followed and Edinburgh castle was captured."

"I must confess," said Bernard. "I didn't know that."

"You aren't believed," said Guillaume and continued on. "On the tenth of July, Balliol abdicated and was exiled to France, a Scottish rebellion ruffled by the rebellion of William Wallace. There was a great fight at the Bridge of Stirling; the English were beaten, and Wallace led his men over the border into Northumberland, where they plundered and burned wherever they went, in revenge for what had been done in Scotland."

"I'm sure this must be leading somewhere," said Bernard, and a small amount of guilt could be seen to be appearing upon his face, a discomfort commencing to take shape.

"In 1298 there was the Battle of Falkirk, where Wallace was

defeated by King Edward. Wallace was executed in 1305, and in 1306, Robert the Bruce, now crowned king of Scotland, came to power and made a stand against the English king. It's then that Robert the Bruce is excommunicated by the pope in 1306, one year before the persecution of the Templars began. With this excommunication came salvation. The papal decree that outlawed the Knights Templar was not applicable in Scotland as Robert the Bruce dismissed it. No effort at all was ever made to prosecute the Knighthood in Scotland and this was a major attraction to many Templars in hiding. Though perhaps no longer able to openly call themselves Templars, they appear to have continued to exercise real power in the world. Edward then dies in 1307, en route to Scotland, and the power of sovereignty goes to his son. Suddenly all is quiet and there seems to be a limited peace upon the land. On the morning of Friday the thirteenth of October, 1307, right across the face of France, most of the Templar Knights were captured and put into chains. The knights were tortured, and propaganda was in full swing. A letter dated December twenty-fourth, 1310, was also sent to England, a decisive effort to have arrested the Templars for heresy. In England the letter was not well received, and although King Edward the Second delayed the arrests for as long as he could, they were finally drawn to questioning by unfavourable means. Torture was introduced to the English legal system, while anyone giving aid to Templars were also to be arrested, excommunicated and suitably punished. Templars were given one year to turn themselves in. The king of England happily seized all of the Templar lands and assets, depriving them of necessary support. Scotland therefore became a beacon for the

Templar cause, commitment, and a safe haven for them all."

Guillaume put down the paper in his hand and looked at Bernard. "Furthermore," said Guillaume. "Robert the Bruce was laying siege to Stirling Castle and a year later Edward led an army to relieve it. The year was almost over when Edward came into Scotland with an army of English, Welsh, and Gascons from Aquitaine; but Robert the Bruce was a capable general, Edward the Second was not. The year was 1314, it was June. What can you tell me?"

"What... what am I supposed to say?" asked Bernard.

"I want to know your part," said Guillaume. "I have papers on you; I have reports on the information of your earlier questioning. I simply wish to hear the truth; all of it."

"Do you wish me to boast of my courage, or simply advise of my efforts to remain alive?"

"Your story, as you see it," answered Guillaume.

# Twenty

"Scotland has suffered badly at the hands of the English," said Robert the Bruce. "Damn filthy swine they are. Service; service to God and country; service to the people of this grand land," Robert paced the floor and turned abruptly to face Bernard square in the face. "Your assistance in this matter is greatly appreciated, more so than I can possibly express. The English will piss their pants when they see you coming over the rise, charging their ranks at full speed, banners flying high above, the wind catching the grace of that which you shall display."

"You have served us," said Bernard, "and we simply repay the favour."

"From ships and land you have flocked into our arms, to rally at our side in this, our time of need. You will not be forgotten."

"That, my new friend, will always be doubted," voiced Bernard. "The wheels are in motion and our stand here will go unrecorded. The French King will see to it that we are banished from the books of history where it is within his power to do so. If he should win this fight, hiding behind the English as he does, then the Templar will be no more."

"Don't talk like that," insisted Robert. "The foul stench of such words should serve to denounce the English, but not good men like you. Many people see you as renegades but I see much, much more than that. I see honour in your eyes, honour, courage and great integrity. Edward's armies have harried us for far too long and now it is time to set the record straight."

"If you fail, you'll surely die," said Bernard. "Just like William Wallace."

"He died with honour; I can die like that too," said Robert. "But to live; aye; we must all live, fight like we've never fought before. If we fail then Scotland be damned, but victory will secure our freedom."

"How many fights must you win before freedom can be secured once and for all?"

"This one time," said Robert. "The time is near, the time to turn the tide. Our freedom is in reach."

Robert sat back down opposite Bernard and both took a drink of their tumbler. Alone they were, to speak freely on the coming battle.

"They aren't far from here," said Robert. "I can smell them," he said with a detested smile upon his face. "We shall make a mockery of them."

"Aye, I know it, for only knowledge can be obtained from your courageous words" said Bernard. "What is the latest report on the English?"

"The same," said Robert. "They outnumber us in men and arms, in particular their armour and horse. They are twenty thousand and we are but six. Where they have three thousand mounted, we have but, mmm… possibly five hundred." Robert shook it from his mind. "We are on the eve of battle. Do you have everything you need?"

"With six thousand Scots ready to fight and die, and Templars with mounts ready to enact a surprise charge, we need little else but gravediggers to bury the English dead."

Robert slapped him on the back. "Hah! let the crows have them."

The door suddenly slammed open and a man burst through, the door quickly secured against the cold of the growing night by a squire.

Robert looked at the man and after a second recognised who it was as the light of the open fire illuminated the man's face. Robert was upon his feet and smiling, Bernard quickly stood by his side on seeing that familiarity and great friendship was presented by both.

"This good man, Bernard, is the one and only, Alexander Seton." Bernard knew at once that Seton was a Templar, too, and bestowed greeting upon him.

"I came as soon as I could," said Alexander. "The English are here."

"My report gives their number as being twenty thousand," said Robert.

"Add three thousand more and the number will be closer to the truth," replied Alexander. He looked at Bernard.

"A surcoat with a red cross," said Alexander. "How many men are we?"

"We?" said Bernard with a smile and short laugh.

"You don't expect me to stand by and watch you have all the fun now, do you?" said Alexander.

"Always spoiling for a fight," said Robert, "when not engaged in one."

"My father and close relative, John, looks forward to joining the ranks of the Scots," said Alexander, "as I do in joining with the Knights Templar."

"It would be an honour," said Bernard. "I humbly accept your voluntary assistance," he looked to Robert and back. "It appears that we now number sixty."

"Hmm," said Alexander. "I'd say about fifty more than we need."

"I believe every word of it," said Robert.

"Who else do we have?" asked Alexander.

"As expected, we have the Sinclair's, and Sir Adam Gordon and his associates," said Robert.

"I've found good company then," said Alexander and laughed as he pulled up a chair and sat with Robert and Bernard.

# *Twenty-one*

June 24th, 1314.

Bannockburn was a site to see, six thousand Scots standing opposite more than twenty thousand, an army to put fear into any man, except a Scot.

The opposing armies were two and a half miles from Stirling castle, on the field of battle: Bannockburn.

The Scottish army was made up of almost all foot, armed with spears, battle axes and pikes. The mounted men carried the swords of Scottish legend and face paint was adorned by many to place great fear upon the hearts of the enemy, to unseat their nerves. But the English nerves were relatively steadfast, simply due to their overwhelming number.

Bernard was back behind the hill, hidden from view of the English. With him were some fifty-nine other men, each wearing his surcoat and mail, sword in sheath, horse restrained. Today was the 24th of June, a special day for the Knights Templar, for it was St. John's Day.

"Three months ago, Jacques de Molay was burned at the stake," said Bernard to those that he commanded over, his force of Templar, his knights of valour and great eagerness: it was not for him to inspire the three hundred mounted scots as they prepared themselves for sworn duty. "We shall not forget him this day. The revenge we enact today is for him and the Order we love so much. Not a man amongst you shall fight the slightest below your means. All of you must fight until we are victorious, and if God should decide to turn a blind eye upon us this day, we shall not be discouraged. We will not retreat but fight until the very last. We either live to win or die fighting. The Scottish has taken us in when others have dishonoured us with cold stares and closed doors. This ground has been chosen by Robert the Bruce and for good reason; he is empowered with a vision, one where freedom will be won this very day, and we shall see to it that we provide unconditional assistance in all he seeks."

The speech was suddenly brought to a close as noise came upon them from a flank. Approaching was one hundred Scottish pony boys and camp followers armed with all manner of weapons from pitch forks to clubs, vastly different from the others of their country. Not a single Templar saw reason to mock them.

The pony boys pushed up level with the Templars. Both were as different as apples and oranges; not of the same field; their ponies varied in size and they displayed riding skills somewhat... inferior to those of the Templar.

"These men, here, will be called to battle before us," said Bernard to his band of brothers. "They will see to it that the archers of the English army allow us easy access to the king and his bodyguard."

A boy ran up and stopped beside Bernard. "They're here," said the boy. "Thousands of them."

"Yes," said Bernard. "I can hear them; I can see the ground

shaking as they march into position; their final resting place."

The boy was stunned. "They're so many, we're so few."

"Your army is tested and has no fear," said Bernard.

The boy looked over to the lads on ponies. "We're no match for the English."

"Boy, listen to me," said Bernard. "There's as much courage in that formation of ponies as there is in the entire English army. You'll be riding with the Templar today, along with your Scottish counterparts, and your duty will see to it that the battle is won. Now go about and report to duty; go stand by your fellow man; be ready for action as your other three hundred scots on horse are ready."

Bernard looked Guillaume in the eye.

"The battle raged all day, and apart from the dead and dying, the screams of defeat and those of valour, the two armies displayed great courage, and each was on the brink of exhaustion."

"What happened next?" asked Guillaume, eager to hear more.

The melee between the Scottish and English was ferocious, clutched in fierce fighting, unable to break what seemed to be an extended moment of stalemate.

Robert the Bruce turned to his squire and gave the order. The order was passed on and received by those in hiding behind the hill. The pony boys and other horseman of the Scottish now broke their silence and flung themselves into battle, attacking the English archers, a charge of horse that was unexpected. The

English were now engaged on all sides where it counted the most for the Scottish, and with the greatest of relief Robert gave one of his final orders for the day and unleashed the Knights Templar of their bonds, untying their restraints.

The fury of battle could be seen in all their eyes, as it could within the horses too, mounts and men both ready for battle.

With a sudden impact, the thunderous hooves of horse and men moving into battle, struck the ears of the English as they stopped what they were doing, fear enveloping them all. They could see the banners flying high above the crest of the hill before them, hear the screams of warning and apprehension from nearby comrades, the fear spreading like a wave gone mad.

The Beauseant was unfurled, moving in the wind as though a ballet was being performed; gracious and sublime. The Beauseant was half black and half white, a war standard to dwarf all others, carried by a single man who was known throughout the ranks of the Knights Templar as the bearer of death: the Balcanifer.

The sight of the man and flag above put instant fear into all the hearts of the English army, a sight not to be believed. It was as though a ghost had appeared before them, an apparition too ghastly to look upon. Here in the midst of Edward's army were the most terrifying of all combatants, those men that struck fear into the bravest.

Other banners could also be seen, as though dancing alongside the Beauseant, bodyguards doing their duty, supporting the one and only true semblance of heroism. Edward could now clearly see before him the advantages of the battle being lost, his men beginning to waver with the fear that continued to mount within them all.

The Beauseant, the Beauseant; there it is, flying high, the symbol of good and bad: the good of the Order for all those of Christian faith and the arrival of death to those of Muslim persuasion. In full regalia the knights continued on into battle, the sea of melee before them ceasing, as though a man upon the land had stopped to view the passing of a monstrous beast. Crosses of red filled the sky, flying above the heads of the mounted Grail Knights.

Bernard could be seen to the front as the men pushed on, breaking into battle speed, to thrust themselves into the ranks of English, to force their way into the thick of battle and onwards towards the king himself, to kill and maim his personal bodyguard wherever they might try to defend him. And the shield of protection gave way, the strongest of the strong giving into fear as the common soldier began to flee the scene, screams of death erupting from them as the horses of the Knights Templar continued on into the thick of battle, pushing ever forwards, for Bernard knew well that the battle would be decided by massacring the English army, not by chasing down a solitary man: is it not true that Scottish heritage can only come from 'vigorous activity', and for such activity you need both a seed and an egg: waste not the potential fathers.

The knights seemed to be swallowed up; disappearing from the face of the earth, but their heads could be seen above the enemy as the English continued to withdraw, being routed as easily as one, two, and three.

King Edward turned unto his special knights, five hundred men on horseback, those that he favoured the most, and together, the grip of fear strangling them all, they fled ahead of the English army as those on foot began to be trampled beneath the heavy hooves of the Knights Templar. Each and every one of the English fled the field, completely demoralized to the core.

Never before had Robert the Bruce witnessed such panic before, the fear spreading so far and wide: so fast and with great effect that the Battle of Bannockburn was won in an instant.

The Scottish foot gained so much ground that they soon fell upon the caravan of the English, the enemy's supplies falling into their hands; their baggage, gold, equipment, and armour and arms: this but a simple goal.

And during the onslaught of that afternoon not a single Templar was lost; not a single one beat an eyelid in fear, for they had confronted much worse in the Holy land, having fought in many battles against a far superior army, where their numbers were miniscule in respect. This battle was nothing to them, it was an easy win. With God by their side they had defeated those that tried at every turn to oppress them.

The English fled the scene so quickly that although many thousands of common soldiers were killed, only thirty-eight barons and knights were counted dead on the field as the glorious win was being celebrated.

# Twenty-two

Bernard fell silent and drew some water to his mouth as the men at the table looked upon him. He was a courageous knight.

"You have proved yourself in battle, many times, Bernard," said Guillaume. "I don't see much lying in you, but of others I can't be too sure."

"Others," said Bernard.

"Those of the Knights Templar who confessed."

"You mean to say, those that were tortured into giving false statements, false evidence, and lies of unforgiving acts."

"Please, Bernard, even if just for a moment... see what we see," said Guillaume.

"I've seen reports, too," said Bernard, "of men withdrawing their confessions of sin."

"Ah, yes," said Guillaume. "Within a month of the trial of the Knights Templar having commenced, the date being April of 1310, fifty-four men withdrew their confessions in order to be burned at the stake."

"Better to be burned at the stake then to suffer miserable days at the hands of torturers," said Bernard.

"Even in England, after much refusal to comply with the wishes of King Philip, King Edward did fold to the sway and poor judgement of the pope and had arrested all knights of the Order, having them placed into custody in January of 1308, long before the trial had even begun in France, yet you slipped through the door, so-to-speak. Who gave you aid?"

"Being charged and being tried are two different concerns. But England paid for its poor judgement later on."

"You refer to the battle of Bannockburn. Who aided you in escape?"

"I refer to the battle in question."

"And of your escape? Come now, tell us all."

"There were many lying underground, defending the righteous name of the Templars. I don't know any more than that. I don't know who they were as individuals and could never again find them, even if I tried," said Bernard.

"Very well, you're believed; I wish to speak on that no more, and for now... well; there's no doubt, from what I have seen this day, that it is your belief, with your entire soul, that the trial of the Knights Templar were highly corrupt, extracting untruths from the Templars who had little choice but to admit guilt in many cases and were hence forced to carry out acts which they would normally be forbidden to enact?"

"I have no doubt whatsoever. My brothers were faced with a grave dilemma, right across the face of Europe, in particular, France. They were promised leniency and advised that the torture that loomed so close could be thrust aside, if only they confessed to these ridiculous charges of sodomy, obscenity and heresy. Few knights I knew, inside out, would have cared about dying, but in the mind of some, torture was too heavy a conviction. Torture would have brought about a confessing, regardless, and all would have known this; and so they told a lie in order to save themselves the pain, to ask God for forgiveness later on."

"The trials in England even started before those in France, in October of 1309."

"The dates are meaningless to me."

"Would you agree that the methods of torture were less.... frivolous, than in France?"

"I would not."

"And so you despise the king of France for that?"

"I do," answered Bernard.

"You know... Confessions extracted—."

"Yes Extracted; that's the word exactly."

"Confessions received from the Knights Templar consisted of many, from the 'kiss of shame', to spitting on the cross and denying Christ. There is also talk of idol worship, where a head of three faces was worshipped."

"I think you refer to the one called, Baphomet," said Bernard.

"Ah, so you know of this? What about Baphomet? What can you tell me?" Bernard looked at the walls as Guillaume spoke and saw the reminder once more: the devices of torture. "You have been here awhile now... trust me, you will not be tortured," gave Guillaume of his assurance.

"I'm tired."

"We'll continue. Go on."

"We, the Knights Templar, have been assailed with accusations of idol worship, but that's far from the truth. It's a combination of two Greek words, baphe and metis, and means 'absorption into wisdom'."

"I find it hard to believe that you can relinquish this to me when so many others have refused it."

"No one would refuse it, but it has been hidden. No, no, no... not a secret kept by us from the citizens of the known world, but kept from the citizens by the hand of the inquisition. They wished the knights to be found guilty and so they conjured up another meaning to the name."

"Some might say it meant, Sophia, the Greek goddess of wisdom," said Guillaume.

"Yes, some might say that, but I've also heard of the Atbash Cipher. It's a joke."

"But no one's laughing. Some say that Baphomet is a strong enough indication that the Knights Templar believed that Jesus was a false prophet and that John the Baptist decapitated, and that's the reason you worship the head. Baphomet means, 'baptism of wisdom'."

"No... no, that's not true. I have nothing to hide," insisted Bernard. "The trials have killed off the Templar, and I have nothing to gain from defending the Order."

"Yes you do, you have conviction and memory, and much honour as well. But I also wish to ask you something more, something that might seem... strange."

"Yes; go on.... this whole damn exercise is a waste of time, though the time is yours: and so I tire at your discretion."

"Come, Bernard, for I am almost through. It's something I touched upon earlier. When Jacques de Molay and Geoffrey de Charney were burnt at the stake there was reported to have been a last summons, as though Molay was exacting a spell to enhance the powers of the devil within, that he called upon Pope

Clement and King Philip to join him on account of his death, to join him before the court of God within the year of this, his last day on earth. Pope Clement is dead but the king still lives."

"Can't be a summons for the devil if it's to God's court they are to be called," scoffed Bernard.

"You're right, Bernard. The voice of one's song changes as it passes from ear to ear. What one person hears might not be the same as another."

"And so you think that King Philip is in danger, and furthermore that I should care?"

"It's different than that; more difficult."

"Please, explain this to me."

"It is clear to us here, that the Grand Master of the Order of the Knights of the Temple of Solomon, Jacques de Molay, and his closest subaltern, the Preceptor of Normandy, Geoffroi de Charney, were executed. King Philip had them removed from their prisons without the pope's authorisation and ordered them to be taken to an island on the Seine where they were unjustly burnt at the stake, and with their deaths went all idea of the reforming of the Templar Order. This was carried out in order to wipe out the Militia of the Temple from Europe, by eliminating the head of its military body.

"Several noblemen had spoken out in defence of the Knights Templar, but these pleas had no effect whatsoever. Before Jacques de Molay perished in the flames, he shouted his innocence and declared that the entire Order was innocent, addressing his words to the king and the pope.

"The French King is responsible for the elimination of the Templar Order, and that is very clear, done so in order to have control over all their worldly possessions and wealth. Little, if any, such responsibility should be attributed to the pope himself.

"The King is alive, the pope is dead. The Templars were defamed on a massive scale. It's with these notes of great interest that we now bequeath to you our interest in this... forage for information from you, which has been an invaluable means by which to understand you more fully. And so, in the power invested in me, as exchequer of France, and being of fundamental importance to the people of France, I request from you your undivided assistance, and from such you will receive immediate pardon from all accusations and untruths, and be set upon the road of your choice, to be free as you deserve."

"And what is this all about; what is it that you need of me?"

"Did you kill the pope?"

"I didn't kill the pope: but that does not mean I couldn't do it, for the good of the Order."

They looked around, they believed him wholeheartedly.

"There's no doubting you, Bernard. And so we come to the reason for this... questioning. We need something of you, a favour if you like. We need you to assassinate the king of France."

"Assassinate the king of France?" stammered Bernard. "You wish me to kill the king?"

"Yes," replied Guillaume rather pointedly. "Ricault will go with you. He knows the itinerary of the king and where he's going to be over the next few days. We have an opportunity open to us. Will you accept it; this challenge?"

Bernard thought upon it for a moment and saw that Guillaume had orchestrated the reply to be spoken, rather well.

In Bernard's mind the decision had already been made. Everything put before him was in some way the fault of the king. He fought hard battles and lived through hell, all of it to be brushed aside by the king so that the Templars' wealth could be squandered. The money would be best in the hands of the exchequer, and although he couldn't be relied upon any more than the commoner on the street, he was the better option when stacked against the king himself; he was the better option between the two: the better of two evils.

Bernard looked into the eyes of all around and then glanced at Guillaume. "I accept."

# Twenty-three

29th November, 1314.

Bernard and Ricault stood upon a well-worn track as the carriage they had just climbed down from suddenly took off, the team of horses spurred on, nostrils flaming with mist.

They both watched as the carriage disappeared from view, only a lantern alight upon the front of the carriage allowing it to be seen, and they opened their ears to the forest around them as the dead of night returned to the solace of that bestowed before their abrupt arrival. They both carried a small bundle each: a little food and water; a blanket. Bernard carried a longbow and a sword hung from his hip, and Ricault had a crossbow, one that Bernard hoped he knew how to employ.

Both men knew the characteristics of their weapons, but knowledge and practical application were vastly different beasts to be tamed: a man could not soften a woman with a soft kiss alone. The English Longbow was made from yew and a skilled English longbowman could release between ten and twelve arrows per minute. The longbow could pierce the armour of a knight at ranges of more than two hundred and fifty yards, but took great skill to handle effectively. The string was made from hemp as it was the strongest and least elastic fibre available. The string was soaked in glue as a protection against moisture.

The crossbow, on the other hand, had a wooden stock generally made from yew ash, hazel or elm, and was coated with glue or varnish. The bolt or quarrel was laid in a groove on the top of the stock and the trigger pulled to release the shot. It had a range of three to four hundred yards but could only be shot at a rate of two bolts per minute.

"It makes me homesick," said Bernard. "Oh, to hear the birds singing in the trees as they do."

"I hear no birds."

"I'm being metaphorical."

"Anyway, you can call this home once more, if you like," said Ricault. "With what we can do for you, you'll be able to go where you please, live as you like."

"The gold you've offered is payment enough: for a pauper: I feel as though a peasant once more."

"It's payment you'll only receive if you should succeed," reminded Ricault.

Bernard looked around as they both stood there. "Are we waiting for someone: or something?" asked Bernard.

"Yes," said Ricault as the beginning of sunshine, at that very moment, sprang an unveiling to come; the lighting of the day from across the treetops. And a few birds began to sing. "Ah, there's your birdsong."

"Ah; waiting for the birds," said Bernard. "Look, I thought this would have been rather simple," said Bernard. "Go in through a window, slash the king's throat, and be on our merry way whilst whistling a tune."

"Have you ever been here before, Bernard?"

"No; of course not. What an absurd question. Do I look like the king's mother; do I look as though I tend his fields, his forest, his mood."

"Then you'll have to put your trust in me."

"I think I've put more trust in you and... you know who; to be granted more than you're willing to pay," said Bernard.

"I'm glad that you've taken the advice so far and forgotten 'His' name," said Ricault. "It shows me that you can be trusted above all others."

"Then your interrogation has paid off."

Ricault looked around a little more. "I'm waiting for an invitation, to see if I can get a better hold on where they might be. This forest is property of the king, as you might well appreciate, and it's very large indeed," said Ricault. "So, to change the subject; you think you deserve more than we're paying?"

"It's a simple observation," said Bernard. "Everything I've done was for king and country, for the people of Christendom."

"You've served better than anyone I can think of," said Ricault who suddenly fell silent. "Did you hear that?"

"No," answered Bernard.

"Are you deaf?"

"Maybe my hearing isn't as astute as yours," answered Bernard sarcastically. "You've seen this," and pointed to his right ear, the scar tissue around the inside a reminder of battle, of his courage in Acre: or somewhere else, he couldn't recall.

"You've a good ear remaining," said Ricault. "I suggest you use it. Come; this way," and he stepped off with Bernard close behind.

"What did you hear?"

"It sounded like a horn. It might be the king's party," said Ricault. "He hunts early, some days: rather desperate for a king."

"In the middle of the night?"

"It's early morning...." corrected Ricault, "...or it could have been the wind."

They continued walking and Bernard looked at Ricault. "If we're going to be chasing the wind all morning then we're going to be here all day and for the night."

"Just as well we each have a blanket," said Ricault.

A little breeze then whipped up from nowhere and again a sound could be heard. Bernard looked to Ricault. "I heard it that time."

"You see," said Ricault. "Even God is on our side."

"What amazes me is that you have an insider willing to provide you with the king's location in such a large forest," said Bernard. "If I didn't know any better then I'd have to say that we were the ones being set up."

"That's quite understandable," said Ricault. "The informer has provided me with the knowledge that the king is after a certain prize today, and such a prize is more abundant in one area of this forest than anywhere else."

"What prize?"

"Pig," said Ricault as he looked down at the weapon that Bernard carried. "Where did you learn to use that? I'd heard it's hard to master."

"When I was in Scotland," answered Bernard. "I must admit, however, that I'm nowhere near as good with it as you might expect. The English are true marksmen and this weapon needs much strength to put command over it."

"Then we'll have to get as close as we can," said Ricault.

"You realise that the strength required for the bow is not simply for distance, but for punching through armor."

"Well, a closer target is better skewered," said Ricault as they continued on, a pig bursting from some shrub and scaring the hell out of him.

"I'm better with the bow than you are at holding your nerve," said Bernard.

"I hope so," said Ricault. "We might only get one shot at King Philip. If you miss with the bow then he might become overpoweringly protected."

"I'm hoping to get close enough to use my sword," said Bernard.

"You're crazy," said Ricault. "Maybe you should just use the crossbow. It's much more accurate. You can switch to the longbow afterwards."

"We can use both, together," said Bernard, "at the same time."

"Ah," said Ricault, "There's a small problem with that."

Bernard stopped in his tracks and Ricault continued for several more before turning slowly to face him.

"There's something you're not telling me," said Bernard. "Maybe we should discuss it first."

"It can wait," said Ricault. "We won't know the predicament of our situation until we find where the king is."

"Let's say we've found him," said Bernard. "He's in the open, just over there, a good range for crossbow practice, and we see our opportunity, because the king, himself, is preparing to kill a pig."

"I... I won't be with you, Bernard." Bernard looked at Ricault and seemed to be unmoved by what he said.

"I expected so much," said Bernard. "When Guillaume said that he looked forward to seeing you so that you could both await the announcement of the king's death. I thought then, 'ah; I'm to do the dirty work for myself', and I was right. I suppose I wasn't meant to hear that: I must've had my good ear pointing in your direction."

"Yes, of course, you must have had. Anyway, our assassination plot will be found out if I'm caught," said Ricault. "Once we see the king then you're on your own. You'll have to give me some time to get away before you... carry on with your task."

"I can see now why you insisted on bringing the crossbow; to give me a larger choice in weapons."

"You can do this thing, Bernard," said Ricault. "Do this thing for all of us; for France; for Jacques de Molay. Don't let his final condemnation of King Philip go to waste; don't allow his words to be spurned."

"I'm going to do this thing," said Bernard, "but not for you or France. I'm going to do this thing for me; for all the suffering I have endured; for all the suffering which has been for nothing."

"We won't forget this, Bernard."

"And the world will never know."

"Do you want to be remembered in history as the man who assassinated the king of France?"

"I suppose not," said Bernard. "I've lived an honest life."

"No, Bernard," said Ricault. "You've lived a courageous life, from the moment you were born of your mother."

"Is there courage in the things I have done?" asked Bernard. "Is there true courage in the honouring of wisdom, in the sacrifices made to pledge allegiance to religion? I've done nothing more than serve God."

"You've done more than that, Bernard," said Ricault. "Come on; let's continue."

# Twenty-four

Several hours had passed as the two men continued on through the forest, stepping carefully and slowing their pace as they continued, listening intently for any sign of the king's hunting party. They both felt as though they were rather close when they heard a voice penetrate the forest.

"Get it, Richard," came the sound of a man's voice. "Chase him." The sound of laughter could then be heard, just faintly, as several of the party found something amusing.

"Sounds like Richard has fallen over," said Bernard.

"They're quite close," said Ricault as he moved over towards a tree. "There they are." He pointed. "Just over there."

Bernard looked and saw. "How many do you see?" asked Bernard. "I see seven."

"I see five... no, seven... eight. I see eight," said Ricault.

"Nine," corrected Bernard. "I think I see Richard running back like a hound."

"Ten," added Ricault. "There are ten."

"Is that what you see, or what your spy has told you?" asked Bernard.

"That's what I see."

"So there could be more... the horn you heard earlier would

have been for another party."

"Unless this party we see had split into two," said Ricault, "and has only just come back as one."

"I concur," said Bernard. "The party would have to split up when hunting pigs. I don't see any dogs."

"You will, but not many," said Ricault. "Our 'friend' saw to it that the dogs were fed something last night, but he couldn't incapacitate all of them for fear of cancelling the hunt."

Bernard gave Ricault a rather strange look.

"The driver of our carriage advised me so, prior to departing."

"There's one," said Bernard and he saw a dog running up to and past what was considered to be the one named Richard."

"There'll be three," said Ricault.

"At least you're well informed, if nothing else," said Bernard, watching as the party of ten took a look at the game they'd killed, a pheasant. "I'm supposing that they're all armed and are good shots."

"I would think so," agreed Ricault, feeling the apprehension in Bernard's voice.

Bernard looked into Ricault's eyes. "I'm going to wait for the party to split up again. I think I can then kill them, one by one."

"What?"

"Keep your voice down, Ricault."

Ricault looked towards the party of ten and then back to Bernard. "You wish to kill all of them?"

"If I can kill them, one at a time, so that none of them becomes aware, I'll then get a close shot at the king himself."

"And if you fail with the first shot then the king shall live and we'll never get another opportunity."

Bernard thought about it for a moment. "You might be right. But you have to agree that the best time will be when the team is split into more than one group."

"I agree," said Ricault.

"Which one is your friend?"

Ricault looked out through the forest to the clear ground as the party of ten moved on into a thicker part of the land around.

"I think... yes. Do you see the one near the rear, glancing around? He's a red scarf and a hat with a feather."

"I do," said Bernard. "I'll make sure he lives." Bernard looked to Ricault. "Will you go now?"

"I should," said Ricault, "but... I think I'll stay awhile longer."

"Very well," said Bernard and they slowly, but surely, continued on. "You're the one to face Guillaume, not me."

# Twenty-five

The two men managed to remain downwind from the party and the dogs, and the hunters never knew they were there, until the time for action presented itself, and even then the dogs couldn't appreciate that any danger or threat was near. They were hunting dogs, not dogs bred for combat in a ring, or guard dogs of any description, something that weighed heavily in Bernard's favour, or so he considered.

One of the dogs lifted its head, its ears erect, and it looked bemusedly towards Bernard and Ricault. One of the hunting parties men, Conrad, saw that something had gained the dog's attention.

"Your majesty," said Peter to the king. "I think we have something, over to the left."

"Good," said the king. "Flush it out, Peter. Take Raymond and Isaac with you." The king looked to another behind him. "Pierre; go with them."

Pierre nodded acceptance.

"See Pierre," said Ricault.

"Our accomplice," said Bernard.

"If we're to get help, then it's from him. You watch as he follows the others and stays as close to the rear as he can."

"He'll give us away," said Bernard. "Look at him. He keeps glancing around; he's far too suspicious; he'll give us away before I've had a chance to sup."

"The king's too stupid and arrogant to know anything different; he'll think Pierre is looking for game."

"That's three of them," said Bernard. "I can kill those three quite easily."

"You're crazy," said Ricault. "You're not on a picnic with your wife."

"It's easy for me, forget it. Besides, you should be going now," said Bernard.

"It's not my decision to go," said Ricault. "I've been given instructions by Guillaume, but... I'll stay."

Bernard said: "Stay if you want. Guillaume won't know anything of it."

Ricault looked into his eyes. "Just like the world won't know who it was that assassinated the king of France."

"It's for you to decide whether the world should know or not, for I don't care," said Bernard. "As for the king... with you and Pierre on my side... how can I fail?"

"You're right, of course," said Ricault. "I won't be leaving. I'll stay."

Bernard smiled. "You've just this minute filled me with trust. We're destined for success."

# Twenty-six

Those that remained of the king's party moved ever forward but the other four continued towards Bernard and Ricault.

"They're coming right for us. Our chances of success are diminishing fast. This king will get away," said Ricault.

Bernard looked around. "Quick, give me that small rock." Bernard took the rock from Ricault and flung it away to his flank. The dog's ears pricked up again and it looked over to where the disturbance within a small thicket of brush had gained its attention.

The party moved off towards it and someone from the king's party pointed to the fact that the others had changed direction. The king pointed off towards the north and they wandered off, to try and encircle what it was that Peter was making a move towards.

Bernard said softly: "We can take them out, one at a time. We have to be very quick. I can kill the one in front of your man Pierre. You take the next in line. If Pierre is smart then he'll take out that one up front."

"That's Peter," said Ricault.

Bernard looked Ricault in the face. "I don't care. I care more about Pierre and what he's going to do to help in our situation."

Pierre was once more looking left to right, from the king's party and then out towards Bernard, where he'd seen the dog looking.

"Pierre knows something is up," said Ricault. Bernard gave a wave to Pierre. Ricault almost forgot himself and pulled at Bernard. "What are you doing?"

"No one can see," said Bernard, "and now Pierre knows we're here." Ricault looked towards the four men who were now no more than fifty yards away.

"Get your weapon ready, Ricault," said Bernard.

"I'm ready."

Bernard looked down at the crossbow. "So you are," and with that he notched an arrow.

"Wait," said Ricault. "Pierre is moving towards the man to his front. I see him getting out his knife."

"What's he doing?"

"He's going to kill that man," said Ricault.

"Quickly, we need to change our plan," said Bernard. "You aim for the one in the middle, I'll get Peter."

With not a further word being said the two assassins stood up behind the cover they had. Pierre could see them, for he knew where to look, and within just a few seconds he had closed the gap towards the man in front of him.

Pierre was saying something to him, to draw his attention, pointing off into the distance, a neat little distraction if it worked, but Bernard and Ricault couldn't make it out. Suddenly he plunged his knife into the man's back and covered the gasping mouth with his hand. The man in the centre turned around slowly, having heard something, but no sooner did his eyes fall upon Pierre and his action and he was dead himself. Bernard finished off the last man standing and before he knew it he was walking at a fast pace towards the three dead men, the confused dog, and Pierre: his new friend.

Pierre looked down at the bodies of Isaac and Raymond; he then looked towards the lifeless Peter as Bernard and Ricault drew alongside.

Pierre was looking around. "It's good to see you, Ricault."

"This is Bernard," introduced Ricault.

"I'm happy to meet you," said Pierre. "We don't have much time. The hunting party spreads out when closing on the game, whether pig or not, and we'll be seen soon enough."

"There are three of us now," said Bernard.

"And there's only supposed to be one," pointed out Ricault.

"Yes," said Pierre. "I've done too much, more than I thought I would... I want nothing more to do with this than I have to. I have a family at home."

"You're in it now," said Bernard and quickly retrieved the horn from peter. He put it to his lips and blew hard. The dog sat down beside him and did nothing. "Whose dog is this?"

"The king's, but he has little to do with its feeding or training; servants provide for it," said Pierre. "They'll be here soon. They'll think we have a pig."

"Go to them," instructed Bernard. "Say whatever you think of and take up a position behind them. You'll have to kill again."

"I can do this, but I want to be rewarded," he looked to Ricault for some form of acknowledgement.

Ricault nodded his head. "I'll see it. Guillaume's not going to be happy about all of this killing."

"He'll be satisfied when he has his hands on the Templars' fortune. Go now, Pierre, and we'll be on the flank. Trust us both. We need you to strike first, as you did before."

Pierre nodded his head and ran off towards the other party of six with the dog following close behind him.

# Twenty-seven

King Philip saw Pierre running towards him. "What is it; what's wrong?"

"Nothing, your majesty," said Pierre. "They have several pigs caught up in some brush."

The king looked down at his dog. "Why's this animal not with them?"

"I don't know, your majesty," said Pierre. "Maybe the dog's scared."

"The king's dogs, scared," said Conrad as he laughed. "If I didn't find it funny, I'd find it insolent."

"Peter has asked that we approach from the rear, to prevent the pigs from escaping." The king looked around at the others.

"I must protest," said Marquis. "That would jeopardise the king's safety. Your majesty, we must approach from the flank; any stray shot from the front could be fatal."

The king looked up and bravely said: "No. We'll do as Peter has requested. He has good vision," said Philip.

"I must insist, your majesty, that you stay to the rear. Two parties coming together, towards one another..."

"It will be fine, Marquis," said Philip. "I'll stay to the rear." Pierre felt a sudden rush of fear then, a great amount of apprehension falling over him. If he was to kill the man to the rear then he would have to kill the king himself. This assassination was wrought with misfortune and disaster.

# Twenty-eight

"It won't be long now," said Ricault nervously. "There they are," he pointed.

"I might be deaf," said Bernard, "but I'm not blind."

"They each have a weapon, and you can guarantee they'll be ready to use them."

"We'll do the same as before."

"Wait," said Ricault. "Look; see what I see. King Philip. He's at the rear."

Bernard looked with eyes wide. "I guess your man, Pierre, will be the one to kill the king."

"But will he?" said Ricault.

"That's the plan," said Bernard.

"The plan was for you to assassinate the king, not for Pierre or myself to be involved. Pierre knows these men well. They would have reported the incident as an accident, not as an assassination."

"And it can still be reported as such," said Bernard. "If your man delivers and we kill them all, Pierre can still make a report. No one in their wildest imagination is going to believe that a single man killed a party of nine, to survive without a scratch. Besides, the king's death will never be recorded as an assassination: the people will be denied the truth."

"Your right," said Ricault. "I just hope that Pierre has the insight and the nerve."

"He'll have two things going through his mind at the present; guilt, and the possibility of extra reward for doing good service."

"Aye," said Ricault as he prepared himself for the killing. "We'll do what we can... as before."

# Twenty-nine

Pierre was nervous to say the least and as the party drew towards the area considered to be that to where the pigs were netted, he closed the gap towards the king himself and placed his hand upon the hilt of his knife.

The king suddenly turned upon Pierre. "Where are they?" Pierre quickly removed his hand from the hilt and pointed for the king to see, at the same time several other members of the party looked around to see where Pierre was pointing.

One of the dogs suddenly pricked up its ears and barked before giving a slight growl in the direction of Ricault and Bernard.

"The time is now or never," said Bernard. "Are you ready?"

"I'm ready," said Ricault. "As soon as I hear the twang of your bow, I'll shoot my crossbow."

"Steady now," said Bernard, and he watched breathlessly as Pierre made another move towards the king's rear. "He's almost there."

"Look!" yelled Richard. "I see something."

"The body of one of the others," said Ricault. "Wait for Pierre," insisted Bernard.

Pierre was a step away from the king and removed his knife

from its sheath.

"What is it?" demanded the king as he stopped momentarily in his tracks.

Richard turned and saw Pierre almost falling over the king. "Your majesty! Behind you!" he yelled.

Pierre wasn't expecting the king to stop dead in his tracks and the knife penetrated King Philip, but not with any great force.

A look of horror fell upon the king's face and as he turned with the startled look of pain upon his face, the knife was withdrawn. Pierre then pushed with all his force, the knife slid effortlessly now into the king's gut.

"Murderer!" yelled Richard, his voice echoing throughout the forest, the others turning to see. Richard lifted his weapon and fired it towards Pierre as Bernard and then Ricault fired theirs.

Pierre stood shocked, open mouthed, and then staggered back and fell as the quarrel from Richard's weapon pierced just to the side of his throat, but it was miraculous in its piercing that such a wound could be easily mended, and eager not to draw further attention he remained upon the ground.

To Ricault, Pierre was no 'great' friend, and so thought nothing of it for the present, and as for Bernard - I think we know enough of him to guess what thoughts may be there upon his mind.

The king fell to his knees, grasping his stomach wound as the knife fell from his blood-soaked hands to the forest floor. The two men in front of the king fell dead from the accurate shooting of Bernard and Ricault.

Ferrario couldn't believe his eyes as John Comyns and

Conrad fell dead, with the king himself gasping for air as he looked around, waiting for assistance.

"Marquis; Richard!" yelled Ferrario as he got down upon a knee and brought his bow into line with his eye, pulling back with all his strength the short bow that he carried, an arrow in place and ready to fire. "Protect the king!"

Bernard released his second shot and the arrow pierced the head of Ferrario as easily as a knife slices through water; a third shortly followed but missed its intended target.

An arrow then hit the tree which Ricault and Bernard were beside, Marquis having struck back a retaliatory shot with little effect.

Ricault pulled the string of the crossbow back and slid into place another quarrel. By the time he was ready to fire his second shot, Bernard had a fourth ready to release.

The assassins looked out to their front. King Philip was lying somewhere upon the ground and couldn't be seen. Richard and Marquis were also hiding from view.

"Where are they?" asked Ricault.

"Quiet, fool," scolded Bernard. "Listen." It wasn't long before the gasps of injury and assault came from the king and he then cried for immediate assistance.

"Whoever is alive, I need assistance this minute," cried Philip. "I need assistance, damn it."

Marquis was about to make a move and Richard stopped him. "No, Marquis; wait."

Bernard released his arrow and it swooped towards Richard, the tall grass he was hiding behind shifting in the slight breeze. Richard's head momentarily popped up above the grass before it fell from view.

Bernard lowered his weapon. "If my calculations are right, we have but one target remaining."

"Two," said Ricault. "We also have the king."

"I saw Pierre stab him," said Bernard. "He won't be in any condition to fire an arrow."

"Yes," agreed Ricault. "You're right." Ricault looked out towards where the dead lay. "Marquis... is your name Marquis?"

Marquis was silent for a moment, and then through sheer fear revealed himself from the slight hollow in which he was currently hiding. "Yes; that's my name."

"Am I correct in assuming that you are the assistant to King Philip?" Philip could hear the exchange of words as he lay there in pain.

"Yes," answered Marquis. "That's correct. Who are you?"

"Let's just say that it's an assassin's role in life to know all about his intended target, and not the target to know the assassin; and that furthermore you are not that target, Marquis. All we want is the king."

"I... I can't do that," said Marquis.

"If you give the king up then I will reward you well," said Ricault. "The king is all I wish for. His life for yours."

"Don't listen to him, your fool," said Philip. "I'll have you strung up and tortured, quartered and flayed."

"Do you hear that?" said Bernard. "We are two, you are one. The king will not sit favourably with you by his side. You're nothing to him. Reveal yourself and you will be set free. Put down your weapon."

"No, please," pleaded Philip. "Don't listen to them."

"I hear honesty within your voice," said Marquis and he slowly stood up from where he hid.

Bernard released his fifth and last shot which struck Marquis through the heart. "What! Damn you!" yelled Ricault.

"You hired me for a job and that job is almost done," said Bernard. "Come; let's talk with the king."

# *Thirty*

The two men looked down upon the form of King Philip, lying there upon the forest floor, blood everywhere around his gut wound and Ricault looked briefly around for any sign of Pierre: surely he was dead.

"Kill him now and be done with it," ordered Ricault.

"No, please," said Philip. "I'll make it worth your while, if you keep me alive."

"Look at those eyes," said Bernard. "Tell me, Philip; did you have that same look in your eye when you killed the Templar Grand Master?"

"I didn't kill him," pleaded Philip. I... I wanted to save his life but it was too late... I tried."

"Why do you have to lie like that?" said Bernard.

"Come on; hurry up," insisted Ricault.

"You make me sick," said Bernard. "You filthy swine."

"I'm the king," said Philip.

"You're not my king," said Bernard, and in a flash he withdrew his sword and plunged it into Philip's throat, the gurgling sounds of blood in his throat heard as he drowned in his own fluid.

King Philip was dead. "That's it, the job is done," said

Bernard.

"It is indeed," agreed Ricault. "And now it's time to get the hell out of here before we're found out."

They started walking briskly away from the site of the mayhem but Pierre was moving in the opposite direction, clasping hard to the wound at his throat, on a task of his own; to report the death of the king.

"Look; there goes Pierre. Do you think the king's death will be reported as an assassination?" asked Ricault.

"No; of course not," said Bernard. "It's so much easier to live with the idea that he was killed in a hunting accident and that the culprit was punished accordingly. The last thing the authority would want is for the truth to get out. I just hope that Pierre comes up with a good story in order to save his own neck."

"He will." And as they walked away towards where the carriage had left them, a great number of birds flew overhead amidst their migration, and Bernard could only contemplate where his life was to lead him.